Copyright © 2022 Judith Sonnet

ISBN: 9798351587172

All Rights Reserved Printed in the USA

Cover design by Christy Aldridge

Edited by Makency Hudson

The events, characters, and locations in this book are all fictional. Any resemblance to reality is unintended and coincidental.

WARNING: *No One Rides for Free* is an incredibly disturbing and extreme book. It deals with themes that should and will upset readers, including graphic sequences of rape, sexual humiliation, torture, and gore.

# NO ONE RIDES FOR FREE

For

David Hess

The best there ever was, is, and will be

**NO**

**ONE**

**RIDES**

**FOR FREE**

**An Extreme Horror Novella**

**By Judith Sonnet**

NO ONE RIDES FOR FREE

NO ONE RIDES FOR FREE

PRAISE FOR

*NO ONE RIDE FOR FREE:*

"Brutal, unrelenting, excellent characters, fantastic writing: this piece echoed some of Ed Lee's most morbid moments—how great is that?"

Brian Berry, author of Snow Shark.

"*No One Rides for Free* is fast, gripping, and horrific. If you like extreme horror, definitely check it out. This one is seriously messed up."

Brian Bowyer, author of *Flesh Rehearsal*.

"If you are someone who can handle extreme horror, violence, torture, graphic sexual scenes(...) this is a must read."

John Lynch, author of *The Warrior Retreat*.

"Another great, gruesome book by Judith Sonnet. This is an interesting take on rape and revenge. Very disgusting and explicit but seeking not only to disturb but also to explore the psychology of its characters and their trauma, giving a deeper dimension to the story."

Aiden Messer, author of *Days of Dreams*.

"Just know this book isn't for you if you aren't in the right headspace or can't handle even mild gory horror. But if you want some extreme horror done by a master, this book doesn't disappoint."

A.M. Molloy, author of *South*.

"Great story, totally icky, but has the power of good storytelling. This is extreme, so be prepared, but Judith does a great job of maintaining the dread throughout."

Chris Miller, author of *Dust*.

## NO ONE RIDES FOR FREE

"One of the rare books that made me squirm!"

Jason Nickey, author of *Wreckage*.

"It would make David Hess proud!"

Jonathan Tripp, author of *And All That Could Have Been*

"Yeah. I'm not reading that one. Glad it's doing well, though."

Judith Sonnet's Dad.

NO ONE RIDES FOR FREE

NO ONE RIDES FOR FREE

**The following Book has been rated:**

# X

# NO ONE RIDES FOR FREE

## Chapter One

Jodi Quinn deposited the nozzle into the gas tank and began to fill her car. The vehicle drank like a sailor, and Jodi tried to ignore the steadily rising numbers on the screen. She didn't want to know exactly how much she'd be spending at this stop. If she didn't look at it—or at her bank account—then it was like she had spent nothing at all. Of course, this practice was a temporary solution as it did not keep her from fretting over finances for long.

Jodi looked into the backseat and saw that her son was still asleep. Ralph could sleep through a storm, and he had spent most of the trip curled up with his head resting against his hands. It never failed to surprise her how similar Ralph looked to his late father. Ralph had the same blonde-white hair, sharp chin, and he even had a nearly identical dark mole sitting like a fulfilled wood tick over his lip. Unlike his father–who had died in an auto accident shortly after Poppy was born—Ralph wore his hair long. When he didn't have his hair pinned back into a ponytail, it cascaded like lichen between his jutting shoulder-blades.

Poppy was in the passenger seat, scrolling through her phone aimlessly. Service had been spotty, so Jodi was sure she was catching up now that they were parked at the gas station.

Neither of Jodi's children had inherited her auburn hair, or her freckles. They were both blonde and pale, like their long-dead father. Both of them were in college now too. Poppy was a freshman; Ralph was a junior. They went to *Northanger U*. They had discovered that it contained a budding community of up-and-coming filmmakers and visual artists.

Jodi blamed herself for their shared passion. Raising them without a father, they had spent a lot of time in front of the TV while Jodi worked two thankless jobs. She was still at one of them, only now she was The Manager of *Koch's Groceries*–the hilariously named grocery market had seen better days, but Jodi was managing as best she could. It was hard to pull people into a small-time store when the big chain supermarkets offered so much more, and for cheaper prices.

Still, Jodi had worked her tail off, and her kids had grown up with movies. She remembered throwing Ralph a *Terminator 2* themed party for his eighth birthday, and Poppy had insisted on a cake with Inigo Montoya's iconic exclamation of vengeance written on it in lacey icing. Jodi had had to paraphrase the quote to spare herself from making a bigger cake. Poppy hadn't complained, she was just thankful that Jodi had encouraged their interests in cinema.

Every time Jodi got a Friday night off, she spent it with her kids at the theater. They'd get buttered popcorn, too-big sodas, and they'd watch two films. One picked by Poppy and the other by Ralph. Jodi never knew what was coming out, so she trusted her kids to decide what looked worth seeing. The great thing was that neither kid argued about what the other chose to watch. Poppy enjoyed Ralph's action movies with wide-eyed relish, and Ralph was even man enough to shed a few tears during *Pride and Prejudice.* The more time went by, the more uniformed their tastes became. They began to see eye-to-eye on every movie they watched. When one hated a film, the other agreed. Even on controversial topics, such as their profound detestation of Quintin Tarantino. Or their bizarre appreciation for the *Alien* prequels–which just confused Jodi.

Both of them wanted to direct movies, and they wanted to do it together. Their creative bond was remarkable, and they had already written five scripts in their spare time. Jodi often joked that they would replace the Coen Brothers when they grew up. Only, it didn't quite feel like a joke anymore.

Going to college and studying film together, Jodi felt like she was raising one kid split in half rather than two totally separate human beings. She figured she was lucky that way. So very few siblings got along the way Poppy and Ralph did. Jodi didn't even talk to her sister anymore. When she did, it was awkward and stilted. Beth was an upper-class snob and Jodi was flying by the seat of her pants just to make the bills on time—

*Ca-chuck!*

The gas tank was full. Jodi bit her lower lip as she maneuvered the nozzle out from the car and back into its station. A few droplets landed on her shoes during the procedure. She lifted her left foot and shook it. Pellets of gasoline dotted the sunbaked concrete beneath her.

Jodi knocked on the passenger window and Poppy closed her phone-screen before rolling the glass down.

"What's up?" Poppy asked.

"Does anyone need a potty break?" Jodi asked,

cringing at herself for the infantilized language.

"Nah, I'm good." Poppy said.

"What about your brother?"

Poppy rotated in her seat, reached back, and flicked Ralph's nose. He grumbled and opened his eyes. Apparently, his sleep wasn't as deep as Jodi had supposed.

"What?" Ralph wiped his eyes.

"Need a bathroom?" Jodi asked through the window.

"No." Ralph said and put his head in his hands.

Jodi sighed. These kids had bladders of steel. They never had to pee, even during long road trips. Jodi was not so lucky. After giving birth twice and reaching the age of forty, she felt as if she squirted every time she so much as sneezed.

"Well, I'm going in." Jodi said. "How about snacks? Candy?"

"I'll take an iced tea." Poppy shrugged.

"Same." Ralph yawned.

"Okay. I'll be back." Jodi reached into the pockets of her cargo shorts and handed the car-keys through the window. Poppy took them, reached over, and turned the engine on. She sighed with delight as cool air crept up from the vents and filled the cab.

Jodi tugged at the front of her shirt as she strolled

toward the gas station. The Texas heat was terrible. She was relieved that she had worn shorts and a white tee. Ralph had on a jean jacket and denim pants for some reason–the poor boy would have melted had he left the car. Poppy was dressed as sensibly as her brother, wearing black leggings and a hoodie. The kids sometimes made perfect sense to her, and other times they were like aliens inhabiting human bodies. How could they sit in a car for ten hours, wearing uncomfortable clothes, and not have to pee or stretch their legs at every opportunity? It made no sense.

Northanger University was located in the middle of New Mexico. By Jodi's deductions, they had about five more hours left in their trip. The route that they had taken through Texas had been long, flat, and boring. Jodi was looking forward to the adobe buildings, curving roads, and familiarity of Albuquerque and then Santa-Fe.

*The map said this was the fastest way, but it's so bland it just feels longer,* Jodi thought as she scanned the road ahead. It stretched out for miles, blockaded by desert landscapes. Off in the distance, she saw a towering, rocky-faced mountain. At least it was something...

Jodi walked into the station. A bell tinkled overhead.

She looked toward the desk and saw a Mexican man with a bushy beard and a top knot sitting behind the register. Jodi was astonished by how handsome he was. Usually, gas station attendants were either pimply kids, smoke-stained women, or total shlubs. This guy... was a babe.

He looked up with bright blue eyes and cracked a smile through his whiskers. "Hello." He said. His voice was cragged with maturity. It was like smoke, leaking from a furnace. "How're you today, ma'am?"

Even though her bladder was straining, Jodi took the time to stop by the desk and returned his smile. Of course, she really didn't have time to flirt but maybe she could establish a little something here. She could stop by the station on her way back home for a little something other than gasoline.

Jodi had found herself growing hornier than ever since her kids had moved halfway across the country for school. She hadn't been much for random cocks before her husband died either. Not that she had been a prude, but she had been discerning. Jodi had made up for lost time now that she had the house to herself. She currently enjoyed the company of five different men in the past two years.

Greg with his bent cock and his expert tongue. Stuart with his battle-scarred face and his penchant for piss-play. Lewis with his oily hands—a mechanic by trade—and his tender kisses. Waylon with his country twang and his ability to make her go cross-eyed with his fingers. And then there was George, a quiet and mousy man that could fit his entire fist so far up Jodi's pussy, she felt as if he was tickling her uterus.

None of these men were her 'boyfriends.' She hated the term, and she wasn't interested in the concept either.

Jackson had been the only man for her, in the romantic sense. His tragic death had not only ended his life, but also her concept of love.

Jodi had an active sex-drive, and a vibrator just didn't cut it. So, once the kids moved out the house had become a playpen of sordid sorts. At first, Jodi had invited her men over one-at-a-time, and then two-at-a-time. Now, she was hosting almost bi-weekly orgies, where each man took turns stuffing her, pumping her, filling her, and staining her.

It made this whole trip to New Mexico somewhat bittersweet. Yes, she was going to miss having Poppy and Ralph around, but she was also looking forward to the wet debauchery she had in store for her boy-toys. It would be all the sweeter since there had been an entire summer free of sex.

She looked at the nametag pinned to the man's

pinstriped uniform. His name was Mateo, and he really was a hunk. Up close, his cologne smelled musky and overly sweet.

Jodi squirmed a little as she answered his question: "Oh, I'm fine. Just fine. And you?"

Mateo smiled coyly. He had picked up on her hungry gaze and seemed to reciprocate her lusty stare. "My day's looking up."

She bit her lower lip and giggled girlishly. "Say, do you have a bathroom around here? I really have to go."

She did a little bouncing dance, hoping the movement of her tits was exciting him. Again, she had no time to fool around now, but she wanted him to go ahead and start thinking of her naked. She wanted him to dream of her, to obsess over her. She hoped he'd wonder what she looked like sitting prone on the toilet, naked below the waist and sighing with pleasure. She wanted him to be surprised when she came back into the station a day from now, having dropped her kids off, slept in a hotel, and built up her own expectations.

*Could I convince him to fuck me in the middle of the store? Would anyone even notice? It's so dead out here in the middle of nowhere.*

*Maybe someone would walk in on us.*

*Maybe they'd join—*

The image of a stranger pushing his cock into Jodi's mouth filled her brain, while an imaginary version of Mateo filled her asshole. Both men pumped in and out of her, spit-roasting her between their sturdy rods and grunting like rutting animals as they stoked up their ejaculations. Jodi imagined herself drooling from both her mouth and her cunt as she was filled, vacated, filled, and vacated in rhythmic pulls. She imagined her eyes rolling into her skull so that they were the color of their hot semen and—

Boy, did she really need to release her urges soon!

Jodi had been a celibate woman during the summer while her kids were sleeping under her roof and occupying her time outside of work. And she did love them... but God... the things she wanted to do with her fuckbuddies. It was almost criminal how horny and lusty she was.

"Yeah." Mateo said. "It's actually around the back but..." He blushed. "It ain't very clean. Here..." He stood and pointed a thumb over his shoulder. There was a wooden doorway that led into the employee's section of the station.

*Tempting. Is there a cot back there? Maybe we should forget the whole middle of the store fuck-fest and get up to some truly nasty shit back there—*

## NO ONE RIDES FOR FREE

Jodi smiled and walked around the desk, allowing Mateo to open the door and usher her in. She didn't even consider that this move could have proven fatal. What if he locked the door? Or bashed her over the head, raped her, and killed her? All the while her two children waited in the car outside, wondering why she was taking so long. Jodi wasn't a stupid woman, but she wasn't great at making decisions. Only after he led her down a short hallway and toward the employee bathroom did she reflect on the potentially hazardous possibilities.

The bathroom was clean, but that wasn't saying much considering the low standards of gas station toilets.

Mateo opened the door and stepped aside. Jodi smiled and brushed against him as she walked in. She considered leaving the door open and plopping herself on the toilet in front of his shocked and curious eyes. That would really give Mateo a show! Of course, she chickened out and said, "thanks, hon", before pushing the door shut and locking it.

After peeing, wiping, and flushing, Jodi looked at herself in the mirror as she washed her hands. Despite the miles traveled, she looked stunning. Her face was clean, and her hair was curly and thick, and it hung over her shoulders in curtains. Her freckles looked splotchy and deep, especially around her sharpened nose. Her arms were strong, and her stomach was toned. She attended to her body, knowing how easy it was to let things slip the older one became.

*I'll be Mr. Mateo's wet dream tonight.*

Jodi grinned devilishly as she opened the door.

He was waiting just outside the door for her, a boyish smile on his face. "All better?" He asked.

"Much." Jodi paused. "Listen, I'll be back by tomorrow. Are you... working?"

"No." Mateo frowned.

Jodi returned the expression.

"But," Mateo's face broke into a grin, "I don't have any plans tomorrow if you—"

Jodi reached a wet hand out and grazed his chest. "I'm gonna grab some goodies for the road. Why don't you put your phone number on a receipt for me?" She asked.

She walked past him and toward the station. While she perused the racks of snacks and soda-drinks, Mateo waited behind the cash register and watched. She made sure to move slowly and purposefully, allowing him to dig his eyes into her slopes and curves. She looked over her shoulder and caught his eye, and his face went red when she held his gaze. She smiled, reassuring him that it was okay to look. In fact, she wanted him to look. Every motion she made was for his benefit. He was being preyed upon by a beautiful cougar. A woman twenty years his senior, if she guessed his age correctly.

*Good god, I hope he's in his twenties. I don't need that kind of trouble!*

Jodi brought the iced teas and an energy drink up to the counter. She also grabbed a packet of jerky, a box of skittles, and a few bags of chips. After paying, her receipt was printed. Mateo turned it over and scrawled his phone number across it.

Jodi smiled and said, "so, when I come back through town tomorrow, I'll give you a call."

"I'll be counting on it." Mateo said with a wolfish smirk. He scanned her chest, eyeing her tits and the slope of her clavicle in even measure. She realized that he was straining his eyes, keeping them from blinking. He didn't want to have his eyelids between himself and this miraculously sexy woman.

*I've probably made his week.*

Jodi took a good look and was certain that he was *definitely* an adult. Younger than her, for sure, but not too young. Maybe twenty-five. Or even thirty. A very light thirty.

"One more thing, ma'am?" Mateo asked.

"Yes?" She responded.

"W-what's your name?"

Jodi broke into giggles. Mateo joined her. He crossed his hairy arms and chuckled.

"Jodi. Jodi Quinn." She said through her laughter.

"Nice to meet you, Jodi." Mateo said. "That's a pretty name."

*How sweet. How very sweet, please, fuck me until I go blind.* Jodi thought before saying: "I'll call you."

She gathered her goodies, used her hip to pop the door open, and traipsed across the parking lot and back to her car. It was the only vehicle in the lot, which meant that Mateo had no other customers to attend to, so she liked to think that he would risk maybe touching himself beneath the cash register. Maybe he wouldn't be able to stop thinking of Jodi and he'd have to visit that secluded little bathroom in the back of the store and—

Jodi's brain switched from 'slut-mode' to 'mom-mode' as she approached the car. Shifting her snacks from one hand to the other, she pulled her door open, and poured into the driver's seat. The air inside the car was chilly. She felt cold fingers prickle her flesh.

"Sorry, guys." Jodi said. "Momma *really* had to go." She deposited the snacks into Poppy's lap. "Sort through those, okay, hon?"

Jodi turned the dangling key in the ignition. The engine purred comfortably. Sighing contentedly, she began to turn the wheel, driving out of the lot and away from the station.

After cresting over the entryway, she looked over at Poppy and was surprised by what she saw. The young woman was crying. Silently, as if she would be scolded if her tears were caught. Her lower jaw had rumpled inward, and her eyes had turned red. The snacks lay on her lap, untouched, just as they had been when Jodi had dropped them there.

"Darling?" Jodi turned her attention back to the road. She whispered, just in case it was something Ralph didn't need to hear: "Are you okay?"

Poppy sniffled. She said nothing.

"It's okay. You can talk to me."

Poppy remained silent. Jodi chanced a glance over to her girl and watched as Poppy clutched her knees with whitened fingers. She looked panicked now, as if she was experiencing something painful and unpreventable.

"It's okay. Hey, hey... mom's here." Jodi reached over and took Poppy's nearest hand. Her grip turned vice-like. Poppy squeezed so hard that Jodi couldn't help but wince with pain. But she took the hurt... because that was what mommas did. That's why God made mommas.

"What is it, babes? What's the matter?" Jodi asked, growing a little panicked herself.

"They ain't allowed ta talk." A gruff voice rose from the backseat of the car. At first, Jodi thought it was Ralph, Maybe he was quoting a movie, or maybe he was just being a goof.

But when Jodi looked into the rearview mirror and saw The Man, her hopes were shattered. Her heart dropped to the pit of her stomach. Her eyes went hazy, and her tongue became dry. A lump swelled up in her throat and choked her.

She wanted to scream with the shock of it all, but no sound came from her lips. Instead, she stared at The Man with her mouth agape and one hand clutched against the steering wheel. Her other hand—still caught in Poppy's grasp—was slickened with sweat.

The Man was sitting in the backseat and holding a gun to Ralph's head. He was a stranger, the sort of man one pictured when they imagined the worst examples of humanity. His face was round, his yellowed teeth hung out from his curled lips like piss-coated planks, and his eyes were wide and peppered with unstoppable rage. His wiry, gray hairs hung around his ugly dome like a wispy cloud of smoke hovering above a chimney. He had a double chin, a meaty throat, and a face sandpapered with rusty stubble. He was short, stout, and pudgy. He smelled too. It was a repulsive odor that Jodi only noticed now that she *saw* The Man. He smelled of spoiled milk and onion farts; he smelled like sweat and feces. The musk hung over him, reminding her of an abused animal in a shelter.

Only, The Man was incapable of inspiring pity. Just seeing him, Jodi felt as if the world would have been better off had his mother aborted him.

"Oh, God!" Jodi looked back at the road, noticing that she was swerving.

"They ain't allowed ta talk." The Man said again, this time cutting his malicious decree short with a snuffling laugh. His voice was gravely and wet all at once, as if he was gargling something offensive, like his own cum... or blood. "And neither is you. Not yet anyhow. Not 'til I says you can. You hear?"

Jodi nodded, pinching her lips together. She had so many things she wanted to say. She wanted to plead with The Man. She wanted to request that he leave them alone. She wanted to barter with him, her life in exchange for her children. Her wonderful, talented, multifaceted, eerily similar children. They had futures and dreams and goals and... and...

And she pictured the muzzle of his gun pointed directly at Ralph's temple. Ralph was shuddering with silent sobs behind Poppy's seat. Jodi could hear his shaking breaths and horrified whimpers, but she couldn't see him. That terrified her. She needed to make sure that her baby-boy was okay. She felt as if she was abandoning him, simply by watching the road ahead and continuing to drive. What if she stopped the car? What would The Man do? Would he pull the trigger? Would he turn the gun toward Jodi and pop her head like a balloon?

The possibilities were as endless as they were horrifying.

The Man pressed his knees against the back of her seat.

"And before you ask... yes. This is really happenin'." The Man belched.

Chapter Two

Jodi watched the road. So far, The Man hadn't given her any instructions. He had just sat comfortably in the back of his seat, still holding his gun up to Ralph's head. She was brimming with questions, but Jodi didn't dare ask them. She didn't know if this creep was bluffing or if he'd actually blow her son's head off his shoulders. When The Man did finally speak up, it was in a derisive tone.

"Aw. Junior done pissed his pants back here!" He snickered.

Jodi had been driving with only one hand. Poppy was holding on tight to her other, causing it to lose circulation. Pins and needles crawled like spiders up her arm. Jodi wished that her daughter would let go, but she also felt like that was a selfish thought.

## NO ONE RIDES FOR FREE

"Hey, what's yer names?" The Man asked.

No one said anything.

"I said 'what's yer names'? Ya deaf?" He barked and kicked the back of Jodi's seat.

She stammered in response: "J-Jodi. I'm Jodi and t-these are my kids... Poppy an-and Ralph." She wondered if using their real names was a bad idea. Maybe it would inspire kindness if she humanized the children. That way they wouldn't be blank slates to The Man; they'd be real people.

Was he capable of feeling sympathy for others? It took more than just brass balls to hold a gun to someone's head. It took a lack of empathy and a stunning lack of humanity.

"Poppy, huh? Answer me this, Poppy... do you *pop*?" He laughed and leaned forward, filling in the space between mother and daughter. The evil prick held the gun up to Poppy's head and she began to wail. She sounded like an alarm, ringing out for attention early in the morning.

"Get away from her!" Jodi yipped.

The Man swung the gun around and pressed it beneath her chin. He grinned, exposing his stained teeth. His tongue lapped at his sweaty, skin-flaked lips. "Or what, bitch?" He asked, almost matter-of-factly.

Jodi had no retort. The feeling of the gun against her flesh was mortifying. She was aware that all it took was a small amount of pressure, and then the gun would buck in his greasy hand and her brains would decorate the roof of her car.

"Don't hurt our mom!" Ralph yelped.

The Man fell back, vanishing from Jodi's sight and pulling the gun away from her skin. She was relieved, but only for a second. Then, The Man began to yell at Ralph:

"Or what? What are you going to do about it, piss-stain? You gonna fight me, huh? You gonna fight me?"

She heard a wet smack.

Jodi turned around in time to see The Man pull the gun away from Ralph. He had used its handle to bust her son's nose open. Blood hosed out of his nostrils and the skin around the bridge of his nose had crinkled unnaturally.

*It could have been worse.* Jodi thought. *It could be better.* A little voice responded in her head.

"Don't hurt my children!" Jodi demanded while Ralph mewled. His broken nose must have hurt terribly, but he was doing a good job holding back his pain. Maybe he didn't want to give The Man the satisfaction of watching him cry, even though his denim pants were damp with frightened drippings. Maybe he was trying to be strong for the women. A notion that would have been gallant in normal situations, but a natural one at times of high stress.

Jodi turned and glared at the intruder. Her glare could usually wilt a man, but he embraced her hatred with glee.

How old was he? He looked like a geezer, but his bare arms were coiled with muscle. He was wearing a white tank top, which was stained with grime, soot, and dried sweat. His chest hairs were springing up around the edges of his wife beater, and his skin was speckled with crusty sunburn-flakes and inflamed patches of ingrown hair. A fearsome, white pimple sat like a pearl on his left shoulder. The sight of it made her flinch.

He was wearing gym-shorts, and a band of white flesh peeked out between the rim of his shirt and the waistline of his pants. A nest of fur peaked out from the top of his shorts, mossy and damp with fetid sweat.

*Who is he? Where did he come from? I looked around before going into the gas station and... and there was no one there! Where had he come from and why?*

She saw that he had a duffle bag lying at his feet. It was blue and rumpled. The edges of the bag were frayed, but it was zipped shut, so Jodi couldn't even guess at the contents. She had a horrible idea that the bag was either stuffed with stolen money, or valuables from previous victims.

Jodi felt the car pull toward the opposite lane, so she looked away from the gun-wielding maniac and back at the road.

There were no other cars ahead or behind her. The back route had proven lifeless and empty. She was suddenly wishing she had swallowed her pride and taken the toll roads.

*Maybe if you didn't spend so long making goo-goo eyes at that kid at the gas station. Maybe if you didn't wave your butt around for him while you shopped. Maybe if...*

Jodi was suddenly wracked with guilt. What if one second sooner from the store had been the difference between life-and-death? What if she, and the kids, would be driving safely to Northanger now... if only she hadn't flirted so heavily with Mateo.

*No. A strong voice said in Jodi's skull. No. There's no time for 'what ifs' and 'maybes'! Save it for therapy, bitch! All you have to do now is keep your babies safe. Figure out what this creep wants and then get him out of your car.*

Ralph was holding his hands over his busted nose. Jodi looked in the rearview mirror and watched as thin ribbons of cherry-syrup slipped between his fingers and drenched the cuffs of his jean-jacket. He glowered toward The Man but said nothing. There was really nothing to say, Jodi imagined. Her son was surely embarrassed, even though none of this was his fault. Even though no one would blame him for messing his pants, and bleeding once struck.

Poppy had quieted down and was staring vacantly through the windshield. Every now and again, she would hiccup, but she did not cry.

The Man sat back and rubbed his belly. He hiked up his stained shirt, exposing his crusty navel, which looked like a black pit in the center of a white globe. He picked at his belly-button with one hand and tilted the gun from one head to another simultaneously.

Every time the gun was directed toward her, Jodi felt her heart thud in her ears. The panic was at its worst when it was aimed at either of her children. Her knees began to wobble and the lump in her throat expanded like an air-mattress.

Through clenched teeth, Jodi dared to ask a question:

"W-where do you want us to take you?"

The Man looked over at her and scrunched up his face. "You think I's a hitch-hiker? Huh?"

"No. I mean, you must want to go somewhere. You...

you don't want to go where we're going, right?"

The Man snorted. "Where are you going?" His voice made her sick with its grunts and burps.

"C-college." Poppy said with a hiccup. "And, and my roommate is expecting me there tonight—"

The Man nodded before saying: "I don't wanna go there. No. I was never no good at school. Got nothing but 'F's." He laughed. "You know what my teacher said about me in the eighth grade?"

"No." Jodi returned. 'What did they say?"

"She said: 'you won't amount to nuthin'.' Upset me quite a bit. Of course, she weren't the only bitch to piss on me back then. My momma said tha same back at home. So's my classmates, an' even the first gal I piped up. Right after a filled her cunt-tunnel wit' my love-snot, she turn't around and said 'boy, you ain't nothin' to write home about'! I showed her. Cracked her upside the head and... did her up the hole she tolt me not ta use. She done cried her a river when she woke up halfway through all the fun. 'Getcher pecker outta thare!' she hollered! But I ignored her and rutted her dirt-chute 'til I was good and drained." The Man snickered at the memory before turning back to Ralph. "You a virgin?"

Ralph didn't respond. He breathed sharply, blowing bloody bubbles from his nose.

"C'mon. Ain't no reason ta be modest. You laid any pipe yet?"

Ralph jittered in place.

"I asked you a quest--!" The Man began to roar.

"It's okay, Ralph!" Jodi cut in. "You... you can tell him. I won't mind. Neither will Poppy."

They all needed to keep The Man happy. If answering his inane questions was what satiated The Man's horrible appetite... then so be it. As humiliating as it was to hear about her son's sex life, she'd rather he embarrassed than killed.

Ralph looked up into the rearview mirror before glancing over at The Man. He spoke in a low tone, his voice afflicted with pain and rage.

"No." Ralph said.

"No?" The Man laughed. "No? Well, boy! What they even teachin' you in that school there?"

"I haven't found the right person yet." Ralph shrugged.

"Bull!" The Man guffawed. "Back when I was yer age, alls I could put my mind to was splittin' poon and getting blowers. You ain't even had yerself a *maw-job*?"

Ralph looked confused. Jodi was too. The Man may as well have been speaking in tongues to their ears.

"I mean, you even got yerself a handy?"

Ralph paused before saying: "Yeah. I've... I've had that."

"See? I knew it." The Man grinned, as if he had just proven an elusive point. "I knew it. You ain't just been doin' homework up in that fancy college, have you? Tell me about it, son."

"Tell you what?"

"Jesus Christ!" His fury was instant. Jodi feared that if Ralph didn't start answering his questions right away, The Man was bound to lash out at him. "Tell me 'bout the girl! Tell me 'bout what she did ta ya!"

"Oh." Ralph swallowed. He sounded like he was speaking through allergies. "I mean... it wasn't, like, crazy or anything. She's just a friend of mine and we were both stressed out during finals and... and we decided to help each other out. You know? Let off a little steam?"

"You two doin' this regular?"

"No. Only... only once."

"Sheee-yit. Why ain't you bustin' her ass?"

"Oh. Uhm. We... we're just friends." Ralph shrugged. "It wasn't a big deal. Like, it was just for fun. She... she has a boyfriend now and—"

The Man turned away from Ralph and leaned back into the center console. "How about you, Popping-

Poppy? You get any dick on the regular?" He snickered as Poppy mustered up the courage to speak. She was traumatized by The Man's mere existence. He was like a stone being thrown into peaceful waters. Jodi didn't blame Poppy for closing up, but she knew that her daughter needed to humor the brute. Jodi knew that if Poppy didn't, she might not survive.

"You a virgin, girl?" The Man asked.

"N-no." Poppy said.

*I wish I didn't have to know these things about my children.* Jodi thought with agony. *I wish they could enjoy their secrets. I wish... I wish they didn't have to feel ashamed for being normal, sexual, happy people. Adults. They're growing up now, and grown-ups have sex. And this... fiend... he's ruining their happy memories. He's exposing their hidden pieces, and forcing us all to take them in.*

"No? You mean yer cherry's already been *popped*, Poppy?" The Man remarked.

Jodi watched as her daughter blushed.

"Please," Jodi interjected, "just tell us where you want to go, and I'll take you there. You don't have to hurt us, okay?"

"Shuddup." The Man coughed. "I wanna hear about yer boyfriends, Poppy."

"That's my sister, you sick fuck!" Ralph barked.

*Don't antagonize him!* Jodi thought, but it was too late. The Man whirled around and snarled at Ralph, like a dog behind a chain-link fence.

"What're you gonna do about it, boy? I can talk however I fuckin' want to! I'm the one with the gun!" He pointed the weapon toward Ralph's face.

Chapter Three

Jodi thought that he was going to put a bullet in her son's face. The instant The Man raised the gun toward Ralph, she saw the entire life of her boy flash before her eyes. She remembered pushing him out of her body with agonized screams and moans, the feeling of him slipping free from her and crying out for her love. She remembered nursing him, and the way he bit. Jodi hadn't complained, even when he hurt her. It was the price she paid for Ralph's safety and comfort.

She remembered being stern with him when she needed to be. Like when he tracked mud through the house carelessly after playing in the rain, and how uncomfortable he looked in his suit at his father's funeral.

She remembered the way he'd sneak into his sister's room and whisper with her well into the night, both thinking that their mother was asleep and unaware that they were socializing past their bedtime. Neither of them knew that she allowed them their bonding time, and happily so.

She remembered his sullen teenage days, when he grew uncomfortable at her touch. When she managed to embarrass him even when she wasn't saying anything. Yet still, even on those days, they had appreciated one another. She gave Ralph his space, and he gave her the joy of watching him grow into the young man he was today.

She also recalled all the hours they spent as a family at the theater. In the darkness, she'd look away from the screen and toward his slumped shape. She'd listen to him chew popcorn and adjust his straw so he could slurp up the melted ice at the bottom of his almost-empty cup.

She remembered saying goodbye to him outside of his dorm during his first year of college. She remembered crying in his arms when he came home for Christmas.

When The Man pulled the gun away from Ralph's defiant eyes, she breathed a heavy sigh of relief.

*He could have been killed. Over nothing. Over the*

*whims of a crazy bastard... a stranger. Someone that pushed his way into our lives and now refuses to budge. This fucker was going to kill my son, all because he was doing the right thing. All because he was standing up for his sister.*

Jodi wished she could kill The Man. She wanted to cram his gun into his pleading mouth and pull the trigger. An image of his corrupt brains erupting from the back of his sun-scorched skull brought a brief spark of pleasure to her.

She had never wanted to kill anyone before. Jodi couldn't even recall if she had ever even had a violent thought in her head. Even the drunk driver that killed her husband didn't deserve to suffer unjustly. She had wanted him in jail, sure, but she had also wanted him to seek help for his addictions and become a better man in his future.

This wicked man was the exception to her fundamental philosophies. There was no bettering this creep in the back of her car. The Man was evil. Plain and simple. He didn't deserve 'betterment', 'understanding', or 'mercy'. Those words felt weak to Jodi now. She knew exactly what The Man needed.

He needed to die.

"Please," Jodi said, pulling The Man's attention away

## NO ONE RIDES FOR FREE

from Ralph. "Please, just tell me what you want."

"I want you to drive." The Man said.

"W-where?" She hated that he was leading her in conversational circles–like a broken record–but The Man hadn't given her a good answer yet. She doubted he would. As far as any of them knew, the destination didn't seem to matter to this guy. It was all about the journey.

So, he surprised her by saying: "Pull over."

She felt her mouth drop open and her heart thud in her skull. Looking toward the side of the road she saw, much to her chagrin, a parked car. Was it The Man's? Had he left his car out here to wait for his return? Was he going to kill her and take her children hostage in the back of that vehicle?

No. If anything, he'd kill Ralph and keep the girls. It was obvious that The Man was a pervert.

The thought of being raped was repugnant to Jodi, but the thought of Poppy being raped was even worse.

Then, she saw a woman standing by the side of the parked car. She was old and withered. Gray-haired, skeletal, and tanned. Her companion–a balding, mole marked senior citizen–was standing by the front of the vehicle, holding its hood open and coughing as steam rose from inside the car.

*Are we going to help them?* Jodi wondered, but she

knew that The Man was not a charitable sort.

She directed the car toward the side of the desolate road. As she did, she watched The Man in the mirror as he lowered the gun, hiding it from sight. He spoke so everyone in the car could hear him:

"All right, gang. Be cool. Okay?"

*Be cool? How?*

"Just park a ways ahead o' them. And roll down that window, Poppy." The Man said. "You'll be doin' the talkin'."

"M-Me?" Poppy stammered. "What am I supposed to say?"

Jodi craned her head around. The old man was walking toward the car even as she parked it. He smiled and waved, and she could see he was toothless. He was wearing a white tank top, similar to The Man's. If she had to guess, she assumed that the old geezer was a farmer. He was so tanned, he looked as if he was turning into an oak tree.

He sauntered toward the car, moving fast despite his obvious age. Poppy did as she was instructed and rolled her window down.

"Howdy, folks!" The geezer said. "Andy Springfield. Y'all showed up in the nick-o-time, you know? We was worried ain't nobody wou'd be down this way." He hooted.

Poppy seemed to gather her strength before saying: "Well... lucky you. W-what seems to be... the trouble?" Each word came out like a mouse-squeak.

Andy frowned and tapped one of his ears. It was filled with curly gray hairs, which reminded Jodi of a fungus. "Sorry there, darlin'... left my hearin' aid a' home. Yous gotta speak up!"

"What can we do for you?" Poppy asked in a louder and more assertive tone.

"Well, the ol' car seems ta have had it. She's coughin' up awful. My wife said she saw there's a gas station a way back... if'n ya don't mind turnin' 'round."

*We've been there. What if we go back and Mateo's still there? Can he save us from the bad man in the backseat?* Jodi thought with relish. She imagined her crush pounding The Man's face into the dirt and stomping on the back of his head until it ruptured. Like a rotten fruit.

"Oh, well," Poppy said, "I dunno. See, we've got a full car and—"

"How about we take yer wife?" The Man said.

"Huh?" Andy asked.

"Yeah. We can squeeze her 'tween me and the young man back here." The Man said, his tone betraying his intent. The hard-of-hearing senior didn't seem to notice the wickedness oozing from The Man's aura though, and so he smiled as he looked over Poppy's head and into the backseat.

*Don't do it. Don't leave your loved one here. Not with him.*

Jodi silently willed for Andy to insist that they would wait around for another car to come through. She hoped he'd somehow catch sight of the gun, know that something was amiss, and call the cops after taking down the license number on Jodi's car. Perhaps he'd notice Ralph's fractured nose, and the blood that coated his face. Maybe he'd see the terror in Jodi and Poppy's wide eyes.

She willed for all of these things to happen, and she was crushed when they didn't. Instead, Andy Springfield smiled and said:

"Yeah! You can take her back to the station an'... an' she can call tha Triple A from there!"

He must have been poor sighted as well as near-deaf, Jodi assumed.

## Chapter Four

Andy went back to his broken truck and returned with his frail wife. Her movements were unsteady, and her beady eyes were squinted against the harsh sun overhead. The prehistoric woman waved politely toward the car, and Jodi lifted a trembling hand out from her window and waved back.

"We're gonna drive away the moment I get 'er." The Man said.

"Which way?" Jodi asked.

"Not back to the fuckin' gas station." The Man chuckled, dashing even more of Jodi's hopes. "You just gun 'er when I tells ya to."

"Why?" Jodi asked.

"So we can get away."

"No, I mean, why are you doing this?" Jodi insisted.

The Man's smile never left his putrid face. She saw a strand of drool hang from a rusty tooth, like a spiderweb. He connected his eyes to hers through the mirror before speaking: "Because... I've got a gun."

Jodi swallowed and looked back toward the road. There were no cars coming, and no one would be helping her. And she was now about to aid in a kidnapping. Who even was this poor woman they were about to abduct?

"Imma ask you a question, ma'am." The Man said, almost kindly. "Do you hate me yet?"

Jodi didn't know how to respond as she gripped the steering wheel with both hands. Her knuckles were flushed white, and her fingers dug into the wheel so hard she was sure it would crack.

"C'mon. I won't punish none o' yer babes fer tellin' truths. Do you hate me?"

"Yes." Jodi admitted.

"Good." The Man said without hesitation. "That's why I do it."

A beat of silence crossed over the car. Ralph shuddered in his seat, holding his blood-smeared hands over his broken nose.

Poppy seemed to have developed a nervous tick. Her

lip leapt up and down over her teeth, as if she was preparing to bite into something tough and chewy. Her lids stayed closed longer than necessary whenever she blinked, as if she expected to wake up from a nightmare every time she opened them.

"I do this because I *love* being hated." The Man sneered.

Andy knocked on the door beside The Man. The Man threw the door open and leveled the gun toward Andy's face. Before anyone could react, he pulled the trigger. The dormant gun suddenly spoke, and its voice was loud.

The bullet chewed through Andy's face. It shredded the skin beneath his left eye, swam through his cranium, and burst out the back of his skull. His aborted brains sloughed out from the fissure and slipped across the road behind him. A map of memories stretched out like egg yolks on the pavement. His brains actually began to *sizzle* in the oppressive heat.

Andy's corpse flopped backward and collided with the ground. His body released several wet noises and gasps, but there was no chance of recovery. The bullet had one job, and it worked well.

The old woman didn't seem capable of processing what had just happened. She froze in place, looking down at her husband with a mixture of shock and disgust. By the time she was conscious enough to scream, The Man reached out and hooked his hand around her wrist. He jerked her into the car, and her head connected with the hardened door frame as she was sucked into the vehicle's interior. She released a muted groan and fell still, draped over The Man's lap. He reached down, grabbed a handful of her shorts, and yanked her the rest of the way in. Her head landed on Ralph's legs, and he screamed at her touch.

Jodi continued to look at the dead body through the mirror beside her. Other than her husband's corpse at the funeral, she had never witnessed death so intimately before. There were no similarities between experiences here. Jodi's expired soulmate had been made up to look presentable and clean in his coffin. His brains hadn't been stretched out in a pink fan behind him. His head hadn't been punched inwards. His arms were put on his chest, not laid out in awkward angles, as if he was trying to make a misshapen snow angel on the ground.

*How long before Andy starts to bloat and swell? How long before the wild animals of the desert find him? How long until he looks less like a human and more like an oily smear, spread across the ground like jam on toast?* Jodi couldn't help but continue to parallel this horrible death with that of her husband's. What if he hadn't been discovered so quickly. How would his body have looked, all twisted and desecrated on the road for hours and hours?

Jodi found herself wishing that The Man had just shot her. The agony and mental torment she was enduring was more than any human could handle. No human was built for this torture, especially an average woman with two nearly-grown children. Her life was made up of small pleasures. The adoration of her fuck buddies, jealous looks from neighbors, and the idolization she received from her babies. She had never known such negativity before now.

Jodi was The Manager of a goddamned grocery store. The worst thing she had to deal with on a bad day was rotten produce and distempered customers. This was pretty far and away from Jodi's worst nightmares.

And she knew it hadn't even reached its peak yet.

*How can things get worse? An innocent man is dead, and his wife is being dragged into the car with you and The Maniac that's been holding you hostage. Things are looking pretty goddamn, motherfucking bad, girlfriend.* Jodi thought with disdain.

That strange little voice came chirping back in response: *You don't even know, Jodi. Things can always get worse.*

The Man broke her from her haze by shouting: "Drive, cunt!" He beat the back of her headrest with an irate fist. "Drive!"

Jodi popped the car into drive and sped away. The wheels seemed to churn beneath her, and she tried her best not to look in the mirror. She didn't want to watch Andy's body as it grew smaller, and smaller, and smaller...

## Chapter Five

The gnarled, ancient woman was mumbling a prayer. She looked around the car, her trust and happiness all broken at once. The Man had propped her up in the middle seat, squeezed in between him and Ralph.

"W-why are you people d-doing this to me?" She eventually asked.

*It's not my fault, lady.* Jodi thought. *I'm just as much a victim as you are. It's his fault. It's The Man with the gun that did this.*

The Man spoke directly into the distressed passenger's ear. "Shut up, you bag!"

She shrank into the seat, withered by his rudeness.

The Man honked with laughter before holding the gun

up so she could look into its barrel.

"You think your hubby could smell the bullet before he died?" He asked.

The old woman began to cry. Tears streamed freely down the chiseled grooves of her cheeks and filled her whiskered mouth. She shook her head and put her hands up to her ears.

"C'mon, man." Ralph mewled. "She's just an old lady. You have to—"

"I don't gotta do a goddamn thang I don't wanna do!" The Man roared.

"Why don't you just take the car and let us all go?" Ralph insisted on arguing with The Man, it seemed.

"'Cuz, I don't want the car, dumbass. I want y'all!" The Man said.

It was as if he had dropped a hammer onto Jodi's head. It was the confirmation of her worst fears.

*He's just doing this for fun. He doesn't need to go anywhere. He just wants to toy with us.*

Jodi wondered once more about the duffle bag laying by his feet. What was in it? Was it a small collection of possessions? Toiletries? She doubted that, based on his horrible hygiene.

Whatever was in the bag, she was certain it meant bad news for everyone in the car. The old woman included.

Ralph continued: "You don't have to do this, sir. You could just let us all go. We won't tell. We don't even know your name or who you are."

"Oh, that sounds like a good deal. Lemme think on that a mite." The Man mocked Ralph with a grin.

"I'm serious. You could get away scot-free. You'd be getting away with murder! Literally!" He said. "Why don't you just—"

"I ain't gonna kill you... lest I gotta." The Man admitted.

There was some relief now. Jodi saw the light at the end of the tunnel.

"Long as y'all do as I says, there ain't gonna be no need fer nobody ta die." He turned toward the old woman. "That includes you too, Granny."

"Anything!" The woman said. "Anything you say... we'll do. Right?" She looked up toward Jodi and Poppy for confirmation.

Jodi nodded. "Anything."

Poppy said nothing. Her eyes had become blank. She was drawing further and further into herself the longer this ordeal progressed.

*She's traumatized. I should be too. We all witnessed a death. A killing! But it's not over yet. I'm not allowed to feel anything until it's over and we're all home safe.* Jodi thought.

"What's yer name, Granny?" The Man asked.

"B-Brenda." The woman said.

"Brenda. We were havin' a conversation 'fore we picked y'all up. We were talkin' about a little thing called 'love'." He laughed.

Brenda flinched.

"You know what love feels like? Know what it's like? Or have you even been loved in a while?" The Man asked. "Yer ol' man, he still got it up?"

"E-excuse me?"

"Could he put his pecker in you still, or was it all soft and squishy? How long's it been since you felt a stiffy?" He asked.

Shocked, Brenda looked around the car for help. She found none. "That... that aspect of our life is..." She began to break into more sobs. The insensitivity of asking her about her sex life right after killing her husband was absurd. "That...that isn't all that love is." Brenda concluded.

"So, you ain't had a hard one in a while, huh?" The Man concluded. "That's okay. Here... here's a little reminder."

Brenda gasped in shock.

Jodi saw The Man lower his shorts in her mirror. The

sight of his stiffened penis rising up from a mophead of untended pubes was shocking, but she reeled in her fear, surprise, and repulsion without drawing The Man's attention toward her.

"Oh, god." Ralph moaned and looked out the window.

"Touch it." The Man commanded.

"No." Brenda responded, clearly disgusted by his penis.

It was a crooked, knobby thing. His organ had inflated with blood, and it still wasn't much to look like. It was like The Man, stout and pudgy, but diminutive and haggard. His uncircumcised skin looked like a purple turtleneck around the bulb of his glans.

He put the gun against her temple and enunciated his demand: "Touch. It."

Brenda shivered and reached toward his member. Her hands were curled with arthritis, and she struggled to get a grip on him. She held his penis, not moving it but holding on as if it was about to run away.

"There. That's what a hard one feels like. You remember it now? That feeling? You remember the way it pulses and jives? The way it's got his own lil' heartbeat? You remember?"

Brenda's weeping began to reach a higher pitch.

*Ninety years old, and she's being raped. God, this is*

*sick. This has to be a nightmare, right? I mean, this can't actually be happening in the back of your car, Jodi. Right? Right?* Jodi's little voice insisted. Unfortunately, it was happening, and there was no denying it. It was happening right behind her. An old woman was being forced at gun-point to handle the gnarled cock of a psychopath. And there was nothing Jodi could do about it.

"Oh, you know how it feels. Yer hubby, did he have a big pecker? Or was his a little shrimpy?" The Man chortled. He leaned in toward Brenda's face and asked: "Am I bigger than he was?"

Brenda shook her head.

"What did you say?" The Man ground the gun against her temple, pressing it in hard.

"No. I mean... I mean... yours is bigger. Uh-huh. Yours is... is much bigger."

"Harder too, right?"

Brenda seethed.

"Say it!"

"Yes. Harder. Much harder."

"I'll bet it is." The Man snarked. He batted her hands away from his junk and said: "Let's see who's got the biggest pole in the car, huh? Ralph, take yours out."

Jodi blinked and looked back at the road stretching

even further ahead of her. Long, sterile, and sightless. Just miles of empty road and emptier desert. As if the only living beings on the planet were trapped in this car.

"What?" Ralph asked, incredulous.

"Pull out yer ding-dong!" The Man growled.

"N-no."

"Do you *want me* to start shooting bitches? Because I will, Ralph! I tolt you, I won't kill anybody lest I gotta, and if you don't do as I say right now... then I'll better *prove* to you how serious this situation is by pluggin' a bitch full-a holes! You *comprende* that shit, you fuckin' *fucker*?"

The car was silent. Then, Jodi heard a jingle as Ralph undid his pants and shuffled them down his thighs. Awkwardly, he lowered his briefs as well. Jodi tried not to look, but she wanted to protect her son. She wished she could throw a sheet over his nude pelvis, but all she could do was glance into the mirror to make sure that The Man wasn't molesting him.

The Man snuffled. "That ain't even a hard one. Yer gonna need to put him up if'n we were gonna compare 'em. Brenda, why don't you give him a little something to help?"

"Please, I don't want to—"

He battered her face with the back of his free hand.

The sound of meat hitting dry meat resounded through the car like a thunderclap. Brenda sniffled and wiped at her nose, mumbling out as her hand touched the spot The Man had beaten. She was already growing a blue bruise on her left cheek.

"You do as yer tolt." The Man said. "Give him a little love, now."

Brenda reached down and grabbed Ralph by the penis. It didn't stiffen.

"You gotta do more than *that*!" The Man said. "You gotta rub it a little. Put a little spit to it! Ain't you never gave yer old fella a handy before?"

"I can't!" Brenda retorted. "I've got the arthritis!"

"Well, shit, girl! Work through the pain! Get him *up*!"

"I can't!" Brenda cried. "Please, just stop this! Please! My God, don't you ever stop?!"

"I said 'get him up'!" The Man roared.

"Please, I'm not...I can't!" Brenda spluttered.

The Man turned toward Jodi, suddenly and quickly. He was like a cobra striking toward a naked leg. He tipped her head back by the hair and put the gun under her chin.

"Drive off the road now!" He spat into her ear. "Drive off the road!"

Jodi, knowing the gun meant business, cranked the

wheel. The car lurched off the road and into the desert. From the backseat, she could hear her son shuffling back into his pants. He was crying again, but softly.

Brenda's tears were frantic and wild. The trauma was like a stone on Jodi's chest, and she knew everyone else felt the same way. Destitute. Lost. Isolated. Not even God could help them now. They were at the mercy of an inhuman monster, and all of them felt his malevolent presence.

The car rocked and jolted across the desert, climbing up hills and stomping over trenches. The dust flew up in front and behind them, clouding Jodi's vision. She kept her foot on the pedal and kept going, knowing she wouldn't be allowed to stop until The Man told her it was okay.

They drove like this for a good, long while.

Jodi began to wonder how far they were from the road. Could it even be seen from where they were now? She doubted it.

The car careened over a small embankment and landed with a choking roar at the bottom of a cleared-out creek bed. Long dried by the summer's heat, not even lizards seemed to thrive in this hellish place. Still, she continued. She turned the wheel and began to drive down the creek's shaft, lurching along.

## NO ONE RIDES FOR FREE

Beside her, Poppy jumped in her seat with each rough step of the journey. She hiccupped again, having sobbed herself into another storm of bodily reactions. Her breath came loose in nasty burps, almost keeping time with the jouncing automobile.

Jodi knew that her daughter would never be the same after this. Poppy had always had a sensitive and careful soul. Unlike her brother, Poppy had been a diligent rule-follower growing up. She lived to please everyone she loved. Sometimes, this was a good thing. Like, when Jodi needed help around the house. Other times, it worried her. The world could be so cruel to naturally good people, and she didn't want others taking advantage of her kindness.

When Poppy and Ralph discussed their movies together, it was clear that Poppy would come up with the ideas, and Ralph would execute them. He was more insistent and willful, and she was more imaginative and giving.

When she was born, Poppy hadn't cried. It was as if she hadn't wanted to bother the doctors or her exhausted mother.

Now, she was making up for lost tears.

They stippled her smooth cheeks. Drool and mucus hung from her orifices. Her eyes had turned pink, and her face was spotted with hives.

The stress of this whole event was having a direct physical effect on Poppy.

*I'll try my best to get us out of this. I will.* Jodi thought. *I will.*

"Stop the car." The Man rasped.

Jodi stepped on the brakes.

When the car halted, it jerked everyone forward as if they were on strings. When they all regained their equilibrium, the dust was settling, revealing a patch of dried vegetation. Gnarled tree roots stuck out from the wall of the creek, and bushes dotted the ground ahead of them. There was no shelter from the sun, and it hit their car like a spotlight.

"Everyone out." The Man said. "Now."

NO ONE RIDES FOR FREE

# WARNING:

The following pages of *No One Rides for Free* are so graphic, disturbing, and depraved... we are legally obliged to give you time to put it down and decide whether or not you want to continue reading. If you read on then you are consenting to witness the horrors ahead... which are, at times, unimaginable. You are also expected to read on at your own risk, knowing full and well that the producers of this book are not responsible for any side effects that you may—or may not—suffer.

If you are at all squeamish, sensitive, or easily offended, we recommend you find a happier story. If you do continue reading and find yourself growing weak with shock, to stave off sickness, fainting, and even death... repeat to yourself:

***It's only a book...***
***It's only a book...***
***It's only a book...***

NO ONE RIDES FOR FREE

## Chapter Six

The Man stayed in the car, prompting his hostages to move out from the vehicle one at a time, just so no one tried to drive away without him. Not that they would get very far in this shallow embankment. Jodi was first. When Poppy exited the car, she rushed over and hugged her mother tightly. The two stood and waited for Ralph to slink free. He joined the family cautiously. Reunited and holding each other, they watched as Brenda crawled out from the backseat on unsteady legs. Her face was puffy with tears and her knotted fingers were clasped together as if she was continuing her prayers from earlier. She stood beside the huddled family, and they waited for their captor to remove himself from the vehicle.

## NO ONE RIDES FOR FREE

When he did, he kept the duffle bag slung over his shoulder–the same shoulder with the rounded pimple, which had so disgusted Jodi when she first took in The Man's horrid appearance.

The Man sloughed his bag off his shoulder and let it fall onto the hood of the car. He crossed his arms, pointing the nose of his gun toward the cloudless sky above him. He stood in contemplative silence before speaking:

"We've got us a problem 'ere, folks." He clicked his tongue back and forth between his yellowed teeth. "Real big problem. You see, I don't wanna kill you. I really don't. I ain't the killin' type, believe it or not." He stared toward Brenda when he said this, as if hoping that she was reliving her husband's brutal murder in her mind. "See, what I's want is *real* simple. You hear? What I want... is to just have a little fun."

"Please, mister." Poppy spoke up, bravely. "Just let us go."

"I will. I will." The Man said. "But first, I want to play with y'all. I want to get a little something. You hear?" He scratched his crotch. It was still hard beneath his shorts.

*Oh, God. Oh, Christ. Oh, Jesus. He's going to rape us. It's happening, and there's nothing I can do to stop it.*

The Man leaned against the hood of the car. He

## NO ONE RIDES FOR FREE

bobbed the gun from one hand to the other before saying: "Brenda failed to get poor Mr. Ralph hard. Brenda, she's no fun. But don't worry, darlin'. You'll get plenty of opportunities to redeem yourself." He flashed the old woman a wink before continuing: "If Brenda can't get Mr. Ralph hard maybe Poppy can."

Dread crept into Jodi's stomach and laid an egg in its pit.

Poppy began to shake her head 'no'. She looked like a frightened rabbit caught in a trap.

Ralph seethed and spat: "You sick fuck!"

The Man fired his gun overhead. The detonation froze everyone's blood. Each victim fell still, watching as smoke streamed from the gun's tip and wavered like a wispy halo around The Man's scabby brow.

He aimed the gun at Poppy and spoke in a chortle: "Go on then, girl. Get yer duds off ya bod."

Poppy shivered, despite the heat. She crossed her arms and looked over to her mother. Jodi's heart broke. She wished she could intervene and stop this madness before it went any further.

*We have to do what he wants. If we don't...*

Jodi nodded grimly.

"I said 'take 'em off'!" The Man yowled.

"Here." Jodi stepped forward. "I'll... I'll help her." She

felt terrible even saying it, but what choice did she have? Her hands trembled as she waited for The Man to respond. Instead of speaking, he nodded his approval and crossed his arms once more.

Tenderly, Jodi stepped toward her daughter and reached out. Poppy blanched and flinched away from her mother's touch, which broke Jodi's heart all over.

"It's... it's okay." Jodi said. It wasn't. It would never be okay again.

She helped Poppy out of her clothes. Naked, the girl crossed an arm over her chest and cupped her privates with a shaking hand. She stared at the ground, mortified by her nudity and by the violation.

"Now, Ralphie, its yer turn." The Man said.

"You won't get away with this." Ralph said. "You can't... you can't treat people like this."

"I'm about tired of arguing with you, boy. Now, you do as yer tolt... or I start putting new holes in yer momma."

Jodi bit her lower lip. She would have gladly sacrificed her life for her kids at this moment, but she knew it wouldn't end with her death. Her children would suffer and suffer until there was nothing left to hurt.

Ralph undid his denim jeans and skinned them down his legs. He yanked his shirt over his head and tossed it onto Poppy's clothes pile. Then, reluctantly, he pulled down his briefs.

Naked, the siblings waited for instruction.

"I want you to start fuckin' each other." The Man said.

Poppy shook violently. Ralph clenched his hands into fists.

"No." Ralph said.

"If you don't start screwing yer sister, Imma do it fer ya."

As terrible as the notion of forced incest was, it seemed pale in comparison to an assault from The Man. So, Jodi gave Ralph a sympathetic look before saying:

"It's okay, Ralph. Ju-just do as he says."

Ralph looked shocked that his mother would approve of such a thing.

Beside him, the old woman began to pray: "God, please, please save us. Save us, Jesus. Take us from here and keep us safe from this demon—" Her voice was low, and her prayer became a mantra. A quiet utterance that fell on deaf ears.

"I-it's okay." Poppy finally said. "I... I'm okay." She stepped toward Ralph and lowered her arms. "Just... pretend I'm someone else, okay?"

Ralph shook his head. He was biting his tongue as tears swelled up from his eyes. He wiped his nose with the back of his hand and grimaced when Poppy reached out and touched his chest.

"Shhh. It's okay. It'll be over soon. You've just gotta... gotta close your eyes and pretend I'm not me."

Jodi looked away from her children and toward The Man. He was licking his lips. His free hand had yanked his shorts down and was now pulling at his prick. It was inflating like a balloon.

"Go on now. Touch her." The Man said.

"Jesus is my savior, and I will love him forever." Brenda continued.

Ralph clenched his eyes closed and reached out with both hands. They fell upon his sister's breasts. He flinched back, as if he had been electrocuted. Poppy took his wrists and held his hands against her chest. She let her breathing do the rest, pushing her flesh against his palms.

Jodi saw that it was having no effect on her son. Half of her was thankful, the other half was concerned. They needed to please The Man, no matter how degrading his requests. This meant life or death, and if her children died...

"Imagine I'm your friend from school. The one that... made you feel good."

Ralph shuddered. More tears and snot drained from his face.

"Just picture that, okay?"

"He ain't biting." The Man said. "Here, maybe I can help." He turned and tugged at the duffle bag. Slowly, he unzipped it. Jodi watched his pimply ass jiggle as he moved, his shorts hanging like a hammock between his hairy knees.

He turned around, pulling the opened bag with him.

Jodi was jolted with shock upon observing the contents inside.

Chapter Seven

The bag was stuffed with sex toys. Purple dildos, curved vibrators, anal beads, rubber balls with whiskers, masks, gags, fake fingers, and even a synthetic fist. Jodi even caught sight of a disconnected rubber mouth with puckered lips. The collection was impressive and terrifying all at once.

The Man spilled the contents of the bag out on the desert floor with several hurried shakes, like a kid breaking out the prize from inside a cereal box. Thick plumes of dust rose up when the toys collided with the ground, reminding Jodi of smog.

Jodi caught sight of an even more threatening object as well, buried among the sex toys, as if it belonged there.

## NO ONE RIDES FOR FREE

A hunting knife with a broad blade and a sharp edge. The knife was tattooed with dried blood.

All the toys had fluids on them. Blood, flakey bits of skin, compost deposits, shit, and even slickened bile. Of course, all of the fluids had been reduced to a sticky film that crackled in the sunlight.

The Man knelt down and fished through the items before pulling up a gleaming, battery operated, vibrating butt-plug. He grinned as he tramped over toward Ralph before unceremoniously nudging the boy's rear with the object.

"Bend over, son!" The Man said. "This'll perk you right up!"

"No!" Ralph hollered.

The butt-plug was black, and the creamy filth on its surface was unmistakable. Someone had shat on it. Probably another victim of The Man and his disturbed whims.

*He's done this before. He'll do it again.* Jodi thought with horror.

The Man leveled the gun toward Ralph's face, and he did as coached. He bent over, putting his hands against his scrawny knees.

"C'mon. Spread 'em! I can't do all the work!" The Man said.

## NO ONE RIDES FOR FREE

Ralph cried as he pried his backside open and yelped when the plug was inserted. The Man pushed it in without even so much as offering to lube it with spit. Jodi felt her son's pain in her own body, like the incessant itching of a phantom limb. She ground her teeth together and wished a violent death upon The Man once more.

The Man pressed a button on the bottom of the plug. The low hum of its vibrations filled the air, colluding with Brenda's prayers.

"There. That oughta help!" The Man seemed proud of himself, as if he had just solved a mechanical problem. He stepped back and stood by his pile of dirty treasures. Then, without a word, he reached down and began to massage his cock again.

"Go ahead and give him a suck. That'll help too." He told Poppy.

Obediently, her face slackened with grief, Poppy knelt down on the desert floor and took her brother into her mouth.

Jodi didn't want to watch as Poppy groaned against Ralph's penis, so she instead watched Poppy's knees. They were being cut by the rocks beneath them. A sharpened stone jabbed her left knee so hard it looked as if it was crawling up beneath her skin. Blood dribbled out and filled the creases of the floor below her.

"There we go!" The Man declared. "That's more like it!"

Jodi couldn't help it. She looked.

Ralph was still crying. He held his hands over his face with shame and he said: "I'm sorry" as many times as he could. He was standing firm. The stimulation had forced his body to betray him.

## Chapter Eight

He made Ralph fuck Poppy. It was a long and arduous process, but he made it happen.

Poppy was on her hands and knees while her brother rammed in and out of her anus. Jodi cried and moaned, watching as her children were forced to defile each other. The whole time, Ralph wept. Poppy had grown catatonic once more. Her tears never stopped, but she made little to no sounds. Other than the gruesome sound of her being violated, and a few involuntary hiccups, she was muted.

The Man masturbated while watching the act, but he seemed to stop himself every time he came close to finishing. His cockhead was beaded with gummy droplets, but he hadn't cum yet. Jodi wished he would

## NO ONE RIDES FOR FREE

hurry up and get it over with. Maybe, after he had ejaculated, he'd leave them be. She knew it was a reach, but one could hope. And hope was all she had now.

Jodi prayed that she and her children would survive this, and that they could go to therapy to process it. She wished that this Man hadn't destroyed Ralph and Poppy's close relationship and that they could still be brother and sister after this. Maybe, they wouldn't blame each other for what they were being forced to do.

*It doesn't count because it wasn't their choice. He took their power away from them... from all of us.* Jodi thought. *And we can't hate each other because of the things* he *is forcing us to do. Right?*

"This... this is it!" The Man declared. "This... is *love!*"

Ralph pulled out from his sister and leaked onto the ground between her legs. He cried out with shame and horror as he watched a payload of sperm drip out from his red, raw, and mistreated penis. Poppy hadn't been lubricated, so the act had been dry up until Ralph's unfortunate ejaculation.

He scuttled away, leaving Poppy in her all-fours position.

"Oh, God!" He shouted, matching Brenda's prayer. "Oh, God!"

The Man hooted with laughter, taking great delight in

the horror he had inflicted upon the family.

The sun was beginning to drop. The whole process had felt like seconds but had in truth taken a full two hours. Two hours of torment, degradation, and humiliation.

Poppy sat on her haunches and looked down at the white pool her brother had left. She stared into it mournfully, and Jodi knew in her heart that nothing would ever be the same for her and Ralph ever again.

*They loved each other, and you ruined it.* She thought as she turned her gaze back toward the psychopath.

"How do you feel, Poppy?" The Man said. He stepped behind her and put the gun against the top of her dome. "Do you feel... happy?"

Poppy said nothing. She simply stared at the sperm and watched as it crept underneath the pebbles and seeped into the ground. Going from white to translucent in seconds.

"Please, you've had your fun." Jodi said. "Please, let us go now... okay? You said you didn't want to kill us. You just... you just wanted to have a little fun. Well, you've had it, right? Haven't you?"

The Man looked up at Jodi and said: "I lied."

He pulled the trigger.

Poppy's blonde hair leapt as the bullet pounded through her skull. It exited through her chin, driving a hole into its center. Blood fumed out and masked the sperm pile Ralph had left behind.

"No!" Jodi screamed as her daughter pitched forward and lay in a crumpled heap on the ground.

"Oh, Jesus!" Brenda shouted.

Ralph screamed. It was a high-pitched and agonized wail that reminded Jodi of a cat in heat. It was about the loudest and most terrible noise that Jodi had ever heard her son make. A sound drenched in sorrow and hatred and anger all at once.

The Man keened with raspy laughter before stepping away from Poppy. Brown syrup spattered out from her backside; her bowels loosened by her death. A moist burp emitted from Poppy's throat, followed by one final hiccup which serenaded her destruction almost poetically.

Jodi saw stirred brains slip out from the crack in Poppy's skull, like slugs leaking from a busted pot. They wriggled in gray and pink strands, dripping languidly from the wound.

The Man pointed the gun back at Ralph and said: "Fuck her again!"

"W-what?" Ralph asked. His screaming had rubbed his throat raw.

"FUCK HER AGAIN!" The Man demanded.

## NO ONE RIDES FOR FREE

Jodi leapt toward him. Maybe it was foolhardy. He could have fired at Ralph upon noticing her disobedience, but she was blinded by rage and a need for vengeance. Jodi wanted him dead. She wanted The Man to suffer for what he had done to her children.

The Man swiveled and fired, but she jaunted to the left and felt the bullet sear through the air beside her ear. She slammed into him and drove him against the hood of her car.

The gun dropped from his hand and clattered against the desert floor.

Ralph burst into action. He ran toward the madman and began to kick at him as Jodi wrestled him to the ground.

"The gun!" Brenda shouted.

Ralph leapt away and began to scrabble across the ground, going for the gun.

The Man thrust Jodi off of his sweaty body. His pants had fallen to his ankles, so he didn't even attempt to stand. Instead, he wrestled through Jodi's punches and knocked her on her back.

Jodi lay dazed for only a second, but it was long enough for The Man to get what he wanted from the pile of sex toys.

He grabbed Jodi by the hair and lifted her so that she

was sitting on her rump. Then, The Man pressed a knife to her flexing throat.

"Hold it there, son!" The Man declared.

Jodi blinked. When her vision came back to her, she saw that Ralph was holding the gun, but he wasn't aiming it at The Man. Instead, it was pointed skyward.

"Whoa!" The Man said. "Whoa, there... hoss. You'll wanna put that shooter down, right? Else somethin' *real* bad happens ta momma."

The Man pressed the knife against her esophagus. The skin broke and warm blood trickled down into the pit of her clavicle.

"No. No. No!" Ralph said. "No! Let her go!"

"You best put it down, son!" The Man declared with menace.

"Shoot him!" Jodi shouted. "Shoot him, Ralph!" She screamed, even though she knew he wouldn't dare. If he pointed the gun at The Man, then the brute would tear her throat open, and it would be as if Ralph had killed her himself. He couldn't be responsible for his mother's death. The poor young man probably already felt like Poppy's conclusion had —somehow—been his fault. Of course, none of this was his fault. It wasn't, but Jodi knew that the brain didn't often work logically in stressful events.

With sadness etched across his pale face, Ralph dropped the gun.

"Good!" The Man said. "Now... we can get back to business."

*No. No. No. We almost had him! We almost got him!*

"I think you already know what I want you to do." The Man looked over toward Poppy's corpse. "Get fuckin', boy!"

## Chapter Nine

Jodi watched in mute terror as Ralph knelt beside his sister's body. Tenderly, he tried to brush her hair over her decimated face. Her jaw hung loose, broken by the blast that had torn through her head. Blood had drenched the ground beneath her, having flown out of her maw like water from a faucet. The bullet had done its work, but Poppy's job wasn't done yet.

"In the back, like you did last time. I like watchin' you ass-blastin' yer sister." The Man said with a snicker. He held the knife to Jodi's throat still, and his penis nudged the back of her head. Its touch was repugnant.

The sun was low now, and the sky had turned purple. It would be night in a matter of seconds. Jodi wished that the darkness would swallow her.

Ralph positioned himself behind Poppy. Delicately, he lifted her hips so that her rear –caked in solidified and liquid shit—was pointed up to meet his soft cock. Even with the plug still vibrating in his own ass, Ralph's penis refused to respond the way The Man demanded it to.

Brenda was sitting on the ground. Her hands were clenched in supplication, and she had turned her face toward the heavens. Somehow, she still believed that there was a God up there that loved her. Jodi was jealous of her delusions.

"Go on now, boy... get to work!"

Ralph shoved his flaccid organ against his sister's feces-swamped rear. He gagged as he began to hump. There was no chance of him entering her, but he simulated the act regardless.

It worked. The Man's cock grew and grew behind Jodi's head.

Jodi bit into her tongue and watched helplessly as her crying son grinded his flaccid penis against her dead daughter.

"Turn around!" The Man jerked Jodi's head awkwardly. He was still holding the knife, and its hilt dug into her scalp. She shuffled around so that she was facing his dripping organ. His penis was filthy, like the rest of his unwashed body. She noticed red sores along the underside of his shaft, each one aggravated by his rubbing. They were oozing with milky pus, which lubed up his inflated cock.

*You have to do it. You have to make him happy. If you don't... you'll lose your son as well as your daughter—*

At first, she had only been angry. Now, the tragedy of Poppy's senseless demise struck her like a bolt of lightning. Tears—fresh and red—bloomed from her eyes and careened down her cheeks. Bile filled her throat, both in response to the sour smell of The Man's pockmarked prick and the death of Poppy.

Jodi had loved Poppy so. She had loved their 'girl-time', when they went out for fancy dinner and left Ralph at home to play on his Xbox. They would go shopping, eat ice-cream at the mall, and choose a nice place for dinner on those days. Conversations had jounced from boys, movies, and gossip to Poppy's plans for Northanger. Poppy had been nervous about college, and she had spent a lot of time fretting over whether or not she would make friends.

"As long as you have your brother with you, you'll always have a friend." Jodi had once said with a coy smile. It had reassured Poppy, and when they got back home she had hugged Ralph enthusiastically. He acted surprised by the random act of affection, but Jodi knew it had warmed his heart.

The bond between a mother and a child is strong, and once severed, it leaves a hole in the very center of the survivors being. Every memory was now tainted. Even the memory of Poppy hugging Ralph coalesced with her current predicament, and Jodi was forced to watch as the dream-like vision of her son responded to the hug by pulling Poppy down and raping her, right in the living room.

Jodi imagined a terrible sight: brother and sister writhing against each other in painful rapture. She pictured shit leaking out from Poppy's rear and staining the perfect sheen that was supposed to rest over Jodi's memories.

Jodi came back to the present, aware of the sounds behind her. The moist, farting noises produced by Ralph haphazardly thumping against Poppy were as loud as thunderclaps. Ralph was still crying, and he was apologizing as well.

"I'm sorry, Poppy. I'm so, so, so sorry." Ralph was speaking in a whisper, his platitudes reserved for the defiled corpse.

The Man pushed his penis into Jodi's mouth. She gagged again, and this time a rush of slushed vomit cascaded from her mouth. He didn't seem to mind a bile-deluge. In fact, he seemed thrilled by it. He began to pump his hips, pressing his moist meat-rod against the surface of Jodi's tongue. His textures were rancorous and foul.

Behind her, her son continued to sob. His noises ratcheted up as he thrust in-and-out of Poppy. The gentle purr of the plug screwed into his anus wasn't wavering either.

No matter what, Jodi was hearing things that sparked more revulsion inside of her.

Still holding her hair, The Man put the gun against Jodi's temple and began to fuck her face... *hard*. His pelvis collided with her, bruising her nose and clipping her breath short. She moaned with pain as he filled her face with his despair.

"Oh, oh, oh, fuck yeah!" The Man grumbled. "You keep fuckin' that sister o' yours, son! I'll keep mouth fuckin' yer momma!"

"You... *bastard*!" Ralph cried out.

"We're gonna have us a real good fuck-fest, aren't we!" The Man hooted.

"Goddamn you!"

Jodi gulped in a breath. It tasted odorous. The Man's pubic hairs were tickling her nose, and she was dimly aware that something was *crawling* in his nest. Lice. Small little pepper-seeds that squirmed and drank in his pubic mound. Happy to be nestled deep in the thatches of uncared for fur above The Man's rotting junk.

*Oh, God. Oh, God.* Jodi was not praying, but she was hoping that *something* would hear her thoughts and come to her aid.

"You like my dick?" The Man asked. "Huh? How good you like it? You think it's tasty? You wanted it all this time, didn't ya? You saw me an' you wanted me?"

Jodi was incapable of speech. Instead, she closed her eyes and wished he would cum already, just to be over and done with it.

"Hey!" He yanked his dick out of her mouth and threw her to the ground. At first, she had figured that he had become displeased with her.

Then, she heard a shout.

Brenda.

She was scaling up one of the creek's walls and was trying to climb to safety.

She was making an escape!

The Man fired his gun for the fourth time that night. The bullet cleaved into Brenda's left leg and dragged her back down the embankment. She scrabbled at the stones as she tumbled, releasing a spray of blood and an awful cry as she went.

Ralph stopped humping Poppy and watched as The Man –his pants still hanging between his hairy legs– tramped across the ditch and toward the suffering geriatric. Brenda was lying on the ground in a fetal ball. She clutched at her bleeding leg, crying and rolling as if she was on fire.

"Did I tell you ta leave? You cunt!" The Man stood over her, holding the gun out toward her head. His other hand gripped his hunting knife tightly. "No! No, I didn't! And I tolt you... if you ain't any fun than you ain't worth living!"

He stooped down and held the knife over his head.

"NO!" Jodi shouted, her mouth filled with vomit and penile pus.

"Stop!" Ralph dropped Poppy and stood up. His pelvis was battered in drying shit.

The sky had finally turned dark. Stars twinkled brightly above them, illuminating the horrible scene.

The Man stabbed Brenda right in the face. The blade swam under her left eye, producing a hot jet-stream of red fluids, which spattered across The Man's heaving chest. He twisted the knife and yanked it loose. It came free with a muddy suction noise, which was followed by a gasp.

Brenda, a cave plowed through her face, began to scream.

"No!" Ralph shouted, but The Man paid him no mind. Instead, he reached down and yanked at Brenda's shirt... tearing it up and exposing her narrow body. Her breasts lay flat atop her chest and her belly was wrinkled and saggy.

He stabbed her right in the sternum. The blade broke loudly through the bones. The noise was like a tree-branch cracking open.

More blood frothed up from the new wound. Gullies of crimson syrup plopped out and sputtered freely along the edge of the weapon as it slid into her.

"Stop. Stop. STOP IT!" Brenda's voice was drunk with agony.

The Man drew the knife up and began to punch it down in quick bursts. The blade carved her belly, slicing the thin flesh and releasing a spool of purple organs and raw innards. A musky aroma lifted up from Brenda's body and filled the air around the remaining victims.

Brenda was twitching, but her screams had run thin. Now, all she could produce were dull and heavy burps. Her mouth was filled with blood. Gore dripped from her unwanted vents. Jodi could see a cloud of blood surrounding her, being piped out of her body from each hole.

The Man stabbed the knife into the ground and put his free hand against one of the more massive wounds. It was like a secondary mouth opened up above her navel.

"Ready or not, Brenda... here I come!" The Man jeered as he pushed his fist through the hole and into her stomach.

Brenda began her protests anew, encouraged by the invasive fist. Flopping, spasmodically, jittering in place and gulping in bloody mouthfuls... she bucked her head back and forth. The Man laid into his arm, pushing it further inside her cavity.

Blood raced up the offending limb and filled the crook of his elbow.

The Man reeled back, towing a tangled knot of squealing tubes up from Brenda's gut. They were wrapped in his fist like spaghetti around a fork.

Ralph wept brazenly.

Jodi felt more vomit rise in her throat.

The Man stood up and stepped back, holding the guts like a leash connected to Brenda's core. She had stopped struggling and her skin had gone snow pale.

He tugged at the organs, and they came free with a rubbery *snap*.

"Sheee-it!" The Man hooted. "That just about does it

fer Brenda!"

He tossed the organs aside. They landed with a wet *plop* on the ground before uncoiling like an orgy of satisfied snakes.

Brenda was still gasping. Despite the monumental amount of torture she had just endured, the woman refused to kick the bucket. The Man appeared miffed by this, until a devilish smile pulled at his lips. Leaving the knife in its spot, he strolled leisurely back to his pile of obscene goodies.

"What are you doing? Leave her alone! Can't you see she's suffering?" Ralph pleaded.

"You keep fuckin' yer sister, boy! In fact, why don't you clean 'er asshole out? She got all shitty!" The Man mocked Ralph before stooping down and selecting his prize, a long string of oil-black anal beads.

"You're sick! You're a sick, demented, evil fucking animal! You... you aren't even human!"

"I've heard it all before. Sticks an' stones, kid. And I'll break yer bones unless you start lickin' that ass clean!"

Whimpering, defeated, and still sobbing, Ralph adjusted himself so that his face was hovering over Poppy's raised rump. Jodi could smell the mess her daughter had made after expiring, and she didn't envy her son his duties.

Ralph pried Poppy's buttocks open, releasing a funky new wave of liquid shit. He sputtered and gagged, sounding exactly like a struggling chainsaw. Squeezing his eyes shut, Ralph opened his mouth and stuck his tongue out. He leaned in close, knowing that The Man would punish him if he didn't do as he was told. Jodi witnessed his body react to the taste as if he had poked his tongue into an electrical outlet. He shook violently and gagged aloud.

"That balloon knot better be fuckin' spotless!" The Man joked as he stepped over Brenda once again. Brenda looked up at him with deflated eyes. She tried to speak, but all Jodi could hear were dank burps and wet expulsions. Her guts divorced from her body; Brenda was growing whiter by the second. Blood hosed freely from her multitude of wounds.

"Imma make a magic trick outta you, hon!" The Man stated, maliciously.

"Puh... lee..." It was the only thing Brenda could say.

The Man hunkered down and began to feed the anal beads into her gaping mouth. Jodi could only guess what they tasted like, but she was certain they had been crammed into many a brutalized body before now. They probably tasted of fecal matter and rectal juices.

The Man piped the beads in steadily, susurrating with

glee as he went about his abhorrent task. Brenda resisted in minimal actions. She shook her head, pinched her eyes shut, and groaned in pain.

In no time at all, her throat bulged as the beads were forced down it. The tail end of the sex toy hung out like a misshapen tongue from Brenda's mouth. The Man let it go, and it dripped down her chin and wavered above the wrinkled surface of her stuffed throat.

The Man scooted backward until he was squatting over her ruptured sternum. Without even a second of hesitation or repugnance at his own foul deeds, The Man dug his clawed hand into Brenda's stomach hole and reached in. He placed a tongue against his cheek and shut his eyes while he worked.

*No.* Jodi thought. *No. He can't be doing what I think he's—*

"Ah-Ha!" The Man vaulted up and began to pull at something his hand had laid purchase upon inside Brenda's body.

Jodi watched with a mortified expression as the anal beads peeking out from Brenda's mouth began to wriggle like a worm before slipping into her mouth and traveling down her throat.

Brenda rattled wildly, pained by the intrusion, the violation, and the humiliation of it all.

## NO ONE RIDES FOR FREE

The Man stood up and proudly held the beads up over his head. Soused in blood and laced with torn tissues, the beads had made a hellish journey down Brenda's esophagus and through her mulched organs.

Jodi could barely believe what she had just watched. It was beyond any crime she had ever read about.

Brenda released one last burbling cough before dying. Her eyes went as white as her face and her arms lay akimbo by her sides.

Satisfied, The Man tossed the anal beads aside. They landed atop Brenda's unspooled intestines. They almost looked like they belonged there.

## NO ONE RIDES FOR FREE

Chapter Ten

In the darkness, Jodi remembered the names of those that had perished. Andy, Brenda, and Poppy. Even though she only knew one of the deceased, Jodi felt each loss. Their lives had been taken so coldly and cruelly; it just wasn't *fair*. It just wasn't fair at all. Jodi seethed with anger and fear.

The Man strolled back across the creek-bed and stood in front of Jodi, his hardened cock wagging like a magistrate's finger over her head.

"Go on, Jodi. Finish 'er up!" He spat her name out like it was a curse.

He was coated in blood. Even in the moonlight, he was as bright as a red traffic light.

Unwillingly, Jodi opened her mouth.

His penis tasted like blood. It filled her maw and began to rub back and forth, undulating over her swollen tongue. Tears caressed her, and so did the urge to bite.

Jodi envisioned severing his most prized possession from him, the way he had taken her happiness away from her. It was just a fantasy; she wouldn't dream of risking Ralph's life in exchange for revenge.

Looking up, Jodi saw his belly stick out above her, nearly obscuring his grinning face. He fingered the trigger of his gun idly, watching her work but threatening her simultaneously. If she made one wrong move, the gun would fire.

"Oh, Jodi. You know how ta treat a fella, don't ya?" The Man mocked her with sadistic mirth. "Maybe I oughta have you take care of yer son the way yer takin' care of me, huh? You'd like that wouldn't you? I saw you watching his peter. You wanted to suck on it, didn't you? Were you... jealous of yer daughter?"

*Fuck you. Fuck you. Fuck you.* Jodi thought.

"I bet if I made him lick yer pussy, you'll jus' scream with joy! I bet yer about as filthy as I am, ain't ya? You dirty fuckin' bit—"

Suddenly, his face fell, and he released a whimper. Then, he howled in pain.

He stumbled around, and Jodi saw—

--the knife jutted out from his neck.

He had left it in the dirt beside Brenda's corpse and

had walked away from it carelessly. While raping Jodi, he hadn't even noticed his error, until it was too late. Until Ralph stood, picked up the weapon and drove it into The Man's fucking neck!

The knife was burrowed deep, but no blood came forth. The weapon was as much a dam as it was an intrusion. It stood out from the left, like a bolt from an incomplete Frankenstein's monster.

He lifted the gun to fire, but Ralph caught him by the wrist and directed the weapon skyward. The Man yanked the trigger, and its shot burst harmlessly above them.

Jodi still had The Man's penis in her mouth.

She knew it was now or never.

Jodi grabbed his hips and pulled him closer, burying his cock deep into her mouth. Then, she bit down *hard*.

"No! NO! NO!" The Man wailed.

Jodi's teeth sunk into his flesh. Blood burst into her mouth, filling it and traveling down her throat. She didn't care about which diseases he may or may not have carried, all she cared about was the fact that *she* was hurting *him*.

Jodi yanked her head back and skinned his penis with her teeth. The meat seemed to slough off the muscle, exposing pink and red tendons and spongy material. Then, Jodi was free of The Man, and The Man was freed from his organ.

He pulled the trigger again, reflexively. The gun was dry. Every bullet in its chamber had been fired, and now he was as weak as a gazelle by a watering hole.

Jodi swished the remains of his rancid cock around in her mouth. She stood up, holding it in. It filled her cheeks and triggered her gag-reflex, but she wasn't ready to be apart from it. Not yet. She strode toward The Man and relished the panic, the confusion, and the fear in his beady eyes. He looked from Ralph to Jodi, hoping that somehow, they would take pity on him.

They didn't. Ralph secured him in his hold, keeping The Man still so that Jodi could approach him.

"Please... please..." The Man whimpered; all his bravado drained from him. His blood was draining out of his pelvis and the skin around the knife had turned a dark blue. "Please... I... I need help. I'm sick. I'm just... I'm just a sick man and I need—"

Jodi spat his penis into his face. It looked like a wet rag, coated in hot gore and sticky blood. It spattered across The Man's visage, clouding over Brenda's blood. It filled his eyes, his nose, and his own blubbering mouth.

The Man began to writhe in Ralph's grasp. His eyes bugged out of his skull, cherry red with his own fluids. He began to sputter, trying to force his own meaty bits out of his oral cavity.

"Puh-puh-puh-*leeeeze*!" The Man cried pathetically.

Jodi clenched her gunk encrusted teeth together and reached out. She grabbed the hilt of the knife and pressed it in deeper. The Man stood still, holding his breath, and glancing down at the protrusion.

"No one rides for free." Jodi said as she pulled the knife out.

It was like tugging the stopper out from a bath. Blood spumed up from the hole in his neck, filling the air beside him with pink mist and red streams. The Man wept as his blood flew away from him and painted the side of the creek bed. It dribbled down his shoulder, iced his chest, and inked the ground below him. Ralph held him still, smiling wide and enjoying the sight of The Man's fluids leaving him.

In a matter of seconds, The Man went pale. His eyes rolled into his skull, and he sank backward. Ralph let him drop abruptly.

The Man lay on the ground, his face twisted with pain. His pelvis looked like a thanksgiving turkey before it was cleaned, and his pants were weighed down by his escaping fluids, and they now sat around his ankles.

He was dead.

He was finally dead...

Epilogue

When Jodi and Ralph walked into the gas-station, Mateo only had a half hour left in his shift. He looked up and was surprised by what he saw. A naked boy and a blood besmirched woman. Both of them stank of death and their eyes were panicked. He didn't even recognize Jodi as the woman that had flirted with him only a few hours ago.

At first glance, he thought the two were zombies. They certainly looked like the undead, with their sallow faces and bloody decorations. After the woman spoke, Mateo was relieved to see that they meant him no harm.

"C-can... can we use your... bathroom?" The woman asked.

Mateo swallowed before saying: "Yeah, it's in the

back."

The woman frowned, looking as if Mateo had somehow offended her. She looked over Mateo's shoulder and toward the door behind him.

*Does this crazy lady know we have an employee bathroom there?* Mateo thought. *How can she? She's never been here before. Has she?*

The woman took the boy by the hand and led him toward the back of the store.

Once they were out of sight, Mateo called the police.

THE END

## Afterword

This book was a challenge to me, and I mean that literally. I told myself that I had ten days to write, edit, and release it. Only ten days. I'm still not sure what the ultimatum was. I just knew it had to be done, and it had to be done fast. Either way, this is one of my shortest, meanest, and fastest books to date. And with that, I want to say thank you to all who endured all of its horrors. You're a brave reader for trudging through this. And if you were offended by it... I'm sorry, but maybe extreme horror just isn't your bag.

Either way, *No One Rides for Free* was inspired by the "rape and revenge" subgenre. Specifically, the films that came out in the wake of Wes Craven's masterwork, *The Last House on the Left*. The influence of *that* movie should be clear to fans. I'd also like to say that the movies *House on the Edge of the Park*, *Naked Vengeance*, *Thriller: A Cruel Picture*, and *The Night*

*Train Murders* all helped inspire this nasty, Grindhouse-esque tale. I wrote this book with the intent of it feeling like an offensive and cruel rape and revenge thriller, without muting the trauma with social commentary and artful dialogue. This book is supposed to make you feel shitty, and bad, and like you need a shower. As someone who was abused before, that's how the world can feel sometimes, and I think it would be disingenuous of me to write a book about this extreme subject while treating it with kids' gloves.

That said, I take my trigger warnings seriously, so I really understand if this one wasn't for you. Don't worry, not all my books are like... *this*. Some of them are even a little fun and tongue-in-cheek. But if *No One Rides for Free* was ever going to work, then it needed to be dreadful. I hope I succeeded, in that respect, in ruining your day.

Now, what's next? I'm re-editing my debut. *We Have Summoned* is a folk horror novel I wrote in 2019 and had published in 2020. It's not nearly as extreme as my other books, but it's still a bloody, depressing, and dark ride with demons, geriatric cultists, and a lot of unique characters. I'm enjoying retracing my steps with it, adding a few more punches, and fixing some of the dialogue so that it sounds like... something a human being would actually say. The original edition fell out of print when the publishers shut down, so it's been sought after by a few fans for a while now. I'm hoping it lives up to expectations!

A few words of thanks, now.

Thank you to Makency Hudson, who is editing *No One Rides for Free* despite my INSANE self-imposed deadline. It was really cool meeting you at Killercon and I'm glad we'll be seeing more of each other at future events!

I'd also like to thank my friend Sawyer, who shares an enthusiasm for all things David Hess and exploitation.

A huge thank you to Heather Boning, who cheered me on and read my updates as I powered through this.

Thank you to everyone that told me that this crazy idea just might work when I posted about it online. The fact that you all believed in me enough to encourage someone to write a book in ten days is… awe inspiring.

Thank you to Rowland Bercy Jr., Daniel J. Volpe, Aron Beauregard, and Carver Pike. You all are the best influences any new writer can look up to!

Thank you to Christy Aldridge, for designing this WONDERFUL cover and for being a real trooper! I can't wait to read *Inbred*!

And thank you to YOU, my dearest readers. For your

support, your kindness, and your constant affirmation. I wouldn't be doing this if it wasn't for you.

With love,
Judith Sonnet.

## CREAM QUEEN
A Paperback Exclusive

### Preamble

This is my confession.

I'm not delivering it in a thinly walled booth in a church. I'm not telling it to an overpaid therapist. I'm not admitting it to any family members or friends. I ain't even putting it in my diary. Instead, I'm writing it out here. Because even though I don't know your names, I want to trust y'all.

I don't know why I developed this fetish.

I didn't have a traumatic childhood memory with pimples, and most psychiatrists seem convinced that childhood woes fuel adult kinks. Pimples were just a part of growing up, and I never got a kick out of popping them in front of my vanity mirror or in my foggy bathroom. My father never had pimples either, so this didn't stem from a desire to resolve any daddy issues, so close that file right now.

I don't know what caused it but... I'm addicted to popping pimples. The more cream I can excrete from a pimple between my fingers, the more I gush. I can fill my pants just from watching a white curd drip out from a busted skin-bump.

*Ugh.* Even just talking about it is getting me all warm and tingly between the thighs. Y'all will have to excuse me in case I get distracted while telling you this tale but... my god. How can even talk about this shit without getting horny?

You know how it is, when you have a specific kink and you can't get off, so it starts infiltrating your thoughts until you feel like it has infected your brain? Like, you start bringing it up into regular conversations without *really* bringing it up, you know? Yeah, you know. Of course, you do. You're in this chatroom. That means you know.

I'm sorry. I'm talking in circles now because... I'm scared of telling this story. I'm aware that some of you will be offended by it. Some of you will be upset and you may even make fun of me. I don't want any of that. But I really, *really* need to tell someone about this. And it needs to be someone who won't recognize me in real life.

Maybe I should tell you about my husband first, because that's when this whole train wreck started.

Yeah, that's good. Let's start there.

**Part One Mathias**

Mathias wasn't the first man I fucked, but he was the first man to make me cum. Even if he didn't know what *exactly* he had done to make it happened.

Mathias asked me to marry him shortly after we graduated from high-school. We weren't interested in college because it seemed too big a financial risk for two kids from the wrong side of the tracks. I was working retail, but Mathias started working at a greasy hamburger joint—I won't tell you which one, but its mascot has a really punch-able face.

He worked hard and long hours, so I tried to make sure he was happy when he came home since I tended to work the morning shift. 'Happy' for Mathias was a quick blowjob, a bubble bath, and maybe some anal. He loved putting his dick up my ass, maybe because it did absolutely *nothing* for me. I wouldn't cum until I got my vibrator out after he had fallen asleep, or before he came home.

Men, for me, were nothing more than machines. They like their routines, and they despise any form of deviation. So, orgasms weren't a requirement for my love. He came home late one Friday night, and he greeted me with a sigh: "It was a busy one." He said, tossing me a take-out bag. He hadn't brought me

anything from work. He knew I loathed the burgers he flipped. They tasted cold in the middle, no matter how long they sizzled on the
grill.

I opened the bag and dug out a container of walnut shrimp noodles. I began to eat voraciously, leaning against the counter dividing our kitchen from our living room. Mathias pulled his hairnet loose and slumped onto our shabby sofa. We lived in a double-wide, parked in the outskirts of a scummy trailer park. The nearest trailer was empty, and the woods sprawled out beside us for acres.

Mathias was tall, scrawny, and he wore his blonde hair long. I'm short, curvy, my hair is cut into a bowl, and I'm so pale you could probably see through me with a flashlight. I rarely went outside, and the clothing store I worked at was kept dark—like a faux-nightclub.

"How is it?" He scratched at his brow. "Delicious." I said. "Wanna fuck tonight?" "Nah," he said. "I mean... sorry. Do you?" "Are you tired?"

"Yeah. I just needs a bath, I think."

A bath sounded good. I continued eating while he traipsed into the bathroom, filled the tub, and relaxed. Eventually, I joined him. We soaked in the water for a while, just chilling and taking in the warm vibes. I thought about lighting a joint, but I really didn't want to get up, leave the bathroom, trail water everywhere, and then have to build a joint. It was too much of a hassle, and we had had enough for the day.

Mathias reached up and scratched at his brow. He had been doing this for a bit, but I had only just noticed it.

"You a'ight?" I asked. "I'm fine." He responded.

"Did ya hit yer head on something?"

"Nah." He affirmed with a frown. "I'm just... I've got a sore spot."

"Poor baby." I cooed. I'm really good at cooing. "Want me to kiss it and make it better?"

Even though he had said he was too tired for sex, I saw his penis rise like a sea monster from the depths of our bath. The pink head of his rod broke through the surface. I had urged on this reaction, just by existing without clothing and using a cute voice. Mathias smirked and said: "I could use a kiss. He could to." He indicated his erection.

I crawled over to his side of the bath and fumbled with him. We kissed, sank down together, and then the water was jiggling with our gyrations. Half-submerged, he glid in easily.

I shut my eyes and tried to feel something... anything.

I was becoming concerned that either I was asexual, or

my husband was just a lousy lay. We had been together for so long, and he had failed to bring me even close to an erupting orgasm. I looked at his face while he humped me, and I found myself disappointed. His eyes were closed, his mouth hung lazily open, and his chin shuddered. Beads of water clung to his face and dripped down his cheeks.

Then, I saw the pimple.

It was what he had been scratching at.

A perfect little cottage-cheese curd, buried just beneath the surface of his forehead. It was small, soft, and puckered. His nail had scratched it red, but he hadn't broken into the skin yet. The pimple sat in the space above his unibrow, like a third eye.

Again, I wish I could tell you what it was about the zit that so attracted me. Suddenly, and without thought, I desired nothing more than to pop it.

I wanted it to break open between my fingers and squirt a white load into my palm.

I felt my sex grow warm and prickly. I trained my eyes on the zit and imagined squeezing it. I pictured Mathias wincing with pain as the pimple expulsed its coiled juices. This very specific image sparked something deep in the center of my pelvis. I rode Mathias's cock, mumbling to myself:

"Yes... yes... pop it... pop it on me..."

Mathias didn't know I was talking about his blemish. He smiled at my word choice and said: "I'll pop all over you, baby."

An innocent enough declaration, but my twisted brain conjured something much different than what he was envisioning. I imagined his face coated in swollen zits. I saw white bulbs overlapping yellowed custard-mounds. I saw them breaking apart as he frantically milked them with his fingers. I saw pus and zit-cream streaking my bare chest. I wondered if it would look like cake frosting if I rubbed his goo into my skin. I wondered if it would feel cold or hot lubing up my vaginal cavern. I began to grow heated and even more excited, and I started to pound my pelvis vigorously against Mathias's thumping prick.

Then, he exploded inside me.

For the first time in my life, I came right along with him,

Those men that say the female orgasm is a myth are so full of shit. I mean, we all already know that, right? I assume I'm not talking to a bunch of incels here but, just in case I am... holy shit, I came so hard I went blind for a solid minute. I lay against Mathias and shuddered as if the temperature had dropped. The bath felt as if it was filled with salty sweat instead of water.

"Was it good for you, hon?" Mathias asked, breathlessly.

I moaned in response.

We fucked like rabbits that night.

The longer Mathias worked at the fast-food joint, the more pimples he grew. It was something in the air there. The fryers, the hamburger grease, the dirty floors, and the snotty condiments. It infected him, and he broke out in acne tumors like a high-schooler. I wanted so badly to disrupt each pimple on his face, but I had to be covert about it. Besides, he was embarrassed of his outbreak, and I didn't want to mortify him by telling him I wanted to collect a shot glass full of his facial fluids and down it like vodka.

I began to understand how Eve must have felt in the Garden of Eden. There was a forbidden fruit in my house, and I wasn't allowed to touch it. Not without some finagling on my part.

I'd pinch his cheek sweetly, hoping he didn't notice I had selected a bud to break between my fingers. When his back was turned, I'd sniff at the creamy deposit I held in the crook of my thumb. I'd lick it, and shudder with rapture. His pimple blubber tasted like a fine oil to me. Harsh and salty and delectable.

When he was asleep, I'd cautiously pop one of the zits on his forehead. It always produced a mixture of snotty drool and red blood. The two tastes combined heavenly.

I wanted so badly for us to play in my filthy pig pin, but I knew he'd be shocked if I confessed what I truly wanted from him. Not his cock, not his heart, and not even his words of affirmation.

I wanted... his pimples.

Desperate for release, I began to search for someone that could please me the way Mathias couldn't...

**Part Two Joseph**

Eventually, that empty trailer beside us became occupied. A boy just past his teens moved in. He was a bachelor, and so we started inviting him over for movies, drinks, and weed. It was nice to have someone our age around, and Joseph and Mathias had a lot in common. Both of them were metal-heads, they both worked in greasy fast-food restaurants, and they both held no other aspirations aside from getting laid and smoking weed. Mathias often bragged about how easily accessible my pussy was, and I could tell Joseph was jealous.

So, I drew him in while Mathias was at work.

I went over to Joseph's trailer and knocked on the

door. He opened it with a surprised expression before saying: "Hey. What's up?"

It was his day off and I could tell he hadn't showered after yesterday's shift. He stank of French fries, burger juices, and nicotine.

He held an unlit cigarette between his hairy lips and his eyes were shadowed with drooping bags. He had stayed up late, probably drinking and smoking. His trailer had a fetid stench to it, and I wondered if all bachelors lived in such squalor. I couldn't complain because filth was the perfect breeding ground for my favorite defects.

"Do you want to fuck me?" I spoke bluntly and I could tell it surprised him. Joseph swirled his cancer stick from one side of his mouth to the other.

"I'm sorry?" Joseph finally said after some hesitancy. I didn't repeat myself. He had heard me.

I popped my hip out and put a hand against the doorframe. I was wearing a short skirt and a halter top. My boobs were pretty much tumbling out in front of me. I bit my lower lip and blinked slowly, waiting for him to come to his senses.

"W-wait, are you being serious?" He plucked his smoke out of his mouth and flicked it by my shoulder.

"Yup." I nodded.

"I mean, what about yer man?" He asked. "You gonna

tell him?" I countered. "Why?"

"Cuz yer hot."

This was a blatant lie. Joseph was a fat boy with a chin like a hairy ball sack. He also had beady eyes and yellowed teeth. Despite these squabbles, Joseph was fortunate enough to have the one feature I desired above all others. He worked in fast food, just like Mathias... and so he had a treasure-trove of pimples and bumps along the surface of his rancid body. Even now, I saw he had one primed up to erupt on the underside of one of his neck flaps. I wanted to lift the flesh and see if there were more curds beneath, like pearls in a skin-oyster.

Joseph beamed sheepishly and stepped aside. I waltzed into his trailer, still keeping my teeth against my lip. He threw the door closed and bolted it, then he crossed his arms and followed my ass with his eyes.

He was hungry for me.

I stripped quickly. I pulled my skirt up, revealing that I hadn't worn panties. He was quick to grab at my butt, holding me with both hands. He spread me open and knelt down, peering at my anus as if there was a treasure inside it.

"Lick me." I commanded, and he obeyed.

Afterward, I gave Joseph what he wanted. I rolled his briefs down and attended to his tiny prick. He came happily, squirting his baby batter across my smiling teeth.

"Oh, wow!" Joseph said, excitedly. "If'n that ain't the best mouthin' I ever did get! Sheee-it!"

I chuckled, wiping my mouth with a hand. His semen tasted salty and bitter. I doubted Joseph ate much fruit.

I watched his heaving body as he wilted onto his ratty sofa. His clothes discarded; his form was on full display. Much to my errant pleasure, he was dotted in pimples. They grew like ticks beneath his arms, in bands across his belly, and under the flaps of his overhanging neck. He smelled too, like stale bread. Joseph was a veritable pus factory.

"What's yer dirtiest fantasy?" I inquired with a lackadaisically yawn. I played it cool, crossing my legs and sitting down in front of him. It was as if Joseph was sitting on the throne, and I was a peasant awaiting his decree.

Joseph thought for a while before answering: "I ain't never done no girl up tha pooper. I'd like to try that."

I chuckled kindly. "No, no... I mean... what's something filthy you'd like someone to do for you? Something you won't even tell nobody 'bout cuz it could embarrass you?" Joseph shrugged. I was asking a lot of him. I retried my tactic, clarifying things for the lard-ass so he knew I was on 'the level'. "I'll tell you my fantasy if you tell me yours." Joseph leaned forward, licking his chapped lips. "You promise you won' tell no un? That you'll keep it 'tween

us?"

"Yeah, sugar. Cross my heart an' shit. Nobody gotta know."

"I always wanted a blumpkin." Joseph confessed.

I knew what he was talking about, and so I shocked him by saying: "Okay. Let's do it."

"Huh?" Joseph's jaw dropped.

"Yeah. I mean, you gotta take a dump?" "Yes. I mean... yeah. I could."

"Then let's do it."

I took him by the penis and led him to his bathroom. The whole time we walked, he muttered "oh, god" on repeat, as if he was already on his way to heaven. When he sat on his toilet, the ground beneath him seemed to creak and groan. The bathroom was moldy, wet, and stank royally. He didn't keep a cannister of air freshener by the toilet, and so the room smelled of decaying farts and the mound of well-used tissue in the trash can beside the john.

He scrunched his face up and squeezed his eyes closed. "You goin'?" I asked, gently massaging his inflatable cock.

"I... I think I'm... a bit stuffed up." He muttered glumly. "Maybe this'll help." I started giving him some wicked head. I moved up and down, slobbering on his ugly fuckstick. I heard him moan and groan above me as I worked, and then I heard the patter of fecal matter dropping into the toilet bowl. His gasses crept into my nose and tickled my gag reflex. Funny, how farts could yuck me out, but I had no problem fantasizing about pimple sucking.

He came as he shat.

"Oh, hot Jesus!" Joseph susurrated. "Jesus! It do feel good cummin' an' shittin' at the same time!"

"You cummin' so much, you'd fill yerself a pint glass, couldn't you!" I declared, stoking his ego.

His eyes swimming with orgasmic bliss, he took a patch of spongy tissue, leaned forward, and wiped his rear. He stood and flushed. I didn't dare look into the bowl lest I wanted to barf up my breakfast, and Joseph's cock suds.

"Geez, I can't believe you jus' came over to do all this." Joseph stated. "Why?"

"I tolt you. It was cuz yer hot—"

"I ain't and you know it. So, it must be you got somethin' you don't want ta be tellin' yer hubby. Yer own filthy little fantasy, huh? You like banging fat boys? Is that it?"

If only my fetish had been so simply. At least, Joseph was proving smarter than I had assumed.

I didn't see any use in beating around the bush, so I told him the truth. "I got myself a fetish, and I ain't had nobody wants to play it out with me. I also ain't been brave 'nough to ask anybody to... to do what I want."

Joseph leaned against the sink. He hadn't washed his hands and didn't seem like he intended to.

"I want," I said, "to have someone pop their pimples in my mouth."

Joseph raised his dandruff lined brows. "Well, that's a new un!" He said.

"Don't make fun!" I crossed my arms and gave him an exaggerated pout. I'm really good at pouting.

"T'aint makin' fun! Jus' never done heard me o' girls liking that." Joseph shook his head. 'T'aint heard of NOBODY done liked that. Plumb new territory, I reckon." "Will ya do it?" I asked with a hint of desperation. "Will you pop 'em in my mouth? It's all I want. Just some juice

and—"

Joseph snorted with revulsion. "Nah, girl. That's sick. I ain't giving you that shit. You may wanna actually talk to yer hubby about this cuz... it ain't right."

## NO ONE RIDES FOR FREE

I couldn't believe his gall. I had just serviced him whilst he excreted, and he had the balls to call me 'sick'? I was humiliated, depressed, and agitated by this turn. I had worked so hard building up to this declaration! I had hoped that Joseph would be my permanent hook-up. I had theorized that he could cultivate a field of pimples from which I could drink. Now, my fantasies were dashed, and to boot, I was being scolded.

Joseph turned toward the mirror and inspected his teeth. All the while, he spoke to me in a demeaning and flat voice:

"You best get yer head looked at, hon. Cuz that ain't no normal fantasy of yours. I swears, I ain't never heard of nuthin' so gross. Not even on the porn sites do they do shit like that! Pimples? Really? Yeah, you come over here and whore yerself up all for some zits? That don't make a lick of sense ta m—"

Joseph was such a loud-mouth, he hadn't even heard me heft up the lid to his toilet tank. I don't think he even noticed I was swinging it through the air. I definitely caught his attention when the heavy, porcelain lid cracked into the back of his skull.

The swing rammed his head forward and against his smudgy bathroom mirror. The glass spiderwebbed and I saw a shard needle through his left eye. Ocular fluids and blood jet-streamed from the injury and hosed the sink.

Joseph made a sound like a hog on a hook. He began to writhe around, clutching at the shard that protruded from his swiveling eyeball.

I battered him against the skull once more. This time, I created a dent along the ridge of his scalp. A curtain of blood draped over his face and the glass fragment was forgotten. Joseph slumped against the closed bathroom door and began to sink to his knees. His flesh jiggled as he descended.

"Pweeze... stahpp..." He mouthed the words around a swollen tongue.

I beat him again. This time, his skull crumbled beneath the weight of the blow. I saw twin squirts of blood shoot out from his ears. His teeth chomped into his tongue, severing it and forcing it to flop onto the floor between his knees.

Joseph fell over dead.

I dropped the lid. It clattered against the ground.

Numbly, I waited for the sound of police sirens. I waited for a phone to ring. I waited for something to happen.

Nothing did.

Bolstered by the lack of immediate consequences, I knelt down beside Joseph and turned his face toward me. The facial damage was painful to observe. It made me flinch just seeing the reflective glass pinning his eyeball to its socket.

Despite my revulsion, there was no way I was going to let an opportunity like this go to waste.

I lifted his neck flap and found a pimple. It was like a little jewel, hidden behind a bundle of ingrown hairs. I squeezed the lumpy skin and watched with glee as the pimple broke. Creamy goo seemed to *flip* out from the spot where the blemish had sat. I hunkered down and licked it up, swirling my greased-up tongue around the puckered pustule wound.

Joseph had thirteen pimples. And millions of blackheads. I tried my best to suck up all I could before going back home.

When Mathias came back to the trailer after work, he offered me a bagged lunch. I told him to put it in the fridge. I didn't want anything infiltrating my stomach, other than the curds I had stolen from Joseph's corpse.

*So tasty...*

**Part Three Paul**

I became like a junkie. A grease-hound. A total slut for pimple sap. I ran from fetish clubs to dive bars, looking for anyone that would satisfy my lust. To avoid suspicion, I amped up the amount of fuckings I gave to Mathias. He loved how ravenous I now was, even though he had no idea I was diverting his attention away from what had become a constant stream of affairs.

I discovered that I wasn't the only one with this gross-out fetish. I do reckon I was the only one in the community that had *killed* for it, though.

Still, I found a lot of men online that didn't mind breaking boils into the mouths of willing cum-dumpsters. So long as they got their nuts pumped, I got my abhorrent fix.

I didn't kill again either. Not for a while, at least.

I set Joseph's trailer on fire after two days without discovery, and the police blamed his death on the flames. I don't even think an autopsy was performed.

Mathias was sad about losing a friend, so I gave him an extra special treat that night. I let him shoot his load into my ass while he choked me. He seemed to really get off on that.

Meanwhile, I was getting off on my own time. I met Paul through the forums.

Not this forum I'm talking to you on... no. You guys wouldn't get what it's like to have a kink like this. You guys like spankings and piss play. None of that is actually gross. I do love talking to you all, because you'd understand before anyone else did. In reality, though, the things I wanted to do couldn't be discussed or conducted here. Or anywhere. So, when Paul reached out and said he had the world's greatest zit and he wanted me to pop it... I was honored.

"Really? Me?" I asked. "Yes." He sent me a selfie.

I had never seen anything like it.

Paul was kind of a ghost on the message boards. While everyone else shared self-made recordings of their pimple-popping exploits, you'd be lucky if Paul gave you so much as a thumb's up or an emoji reaction. So, having him reach out to me made me feel like a very special girl indeed. And seeing his pimple?

Guys, it rocked my world.

The thing was like a soft-ball growing out from the top of his head. It was greasy, shining with moist perspirations. It was red and hot looking, as if it would burn at the touch. The infected fluids inside it had solidified, and I couldn't wait to see how they came out.

I told him I would be there whenever he wanted to meet me. He gave me an address and said:

"Tonight".

I told Mathias I was going to visit my sister, and I left the trailer that evening.

## NO ONE RIDES FOR FREE

The drive to Paul's was short, but it felt like an eternity. My anticipation was killing me. I was also feeling proud of myself. Joseph had made me feel so alone in the world, and now I was actually finding that my fetish wasn't quite the rarity so many people assumed it would be.

When I got to Paul's house, I was surprised. The dude lived in a mansion. I had to ring a bell just to be let through the gates.

The door was opened before I had a chance to knock. A friendly looking man smiled at me and asked:

"Are you here for Mr. Paul's appointment?"

I stammered a quick confirmation before The Manservant whisked me down the hall and toward a back room. The Mansion was gorgeous. Priceless works of art hung from every wall, and there were even a few nude sculptures loitering in the lobby!

"Paul is most pleased," the affluent man said, "that you could make it here so fast. He's been nurturing his affliction for a good while now, and it's about time he had it out! He chose you based on your enthusiasm; you know?"

"Are you... in the group chat?" I asked.

"Heavens no." The butler said, but not rudely. "I mean, Paul just likes me to oversee his activities. He must be *very* careful with who he discusses things with. You never know if you're talking to a genuine fetishist or if its someone looking to make a fool of you online. Paul cannot afford to be made a fool of."

It looked like Paul could afford pretty much whatever he damn well wanted.

"Anyways, he'll be breaking this boil with you tonight, and then he'll grow a new one for another girl to burst. It's a cycle he's been participating in for decades. Are you excited, madam? Do you need any lubricant?"

"N-no." I returned, meekly. I was, frankly, embarrassed by the question.

The kindly butler threw open a set of double-doors and exposed a room I can only describe as a 'murder floor'. The walls, carpet, and ceiling were lined with plastic sheets. Paul was lying on a table, stark naked. His penis lazily bobbed between his thighs, filled and ready.

Paul looked up and gave me a warm smile. His pimple was even more spectacular in person. A small dot of white custard peeked out from the apex of the mammoth zit.

"You can leave your clothing with me, madam." The butler said.

I stripped, already so excited it looked as if I had slimed my panties. I handed my folded garments to the butler, and he closed the doors behind him on his way out.

Steadily, I walked toward Paul.

"Do you like it?" He asked with a slur. He reached up and touched the massive bump. "It hurts, princess. Can you make it stop hurting?" He spoke in an infantilized tone. "Please?"

"Oh, yessir. I'll hop to it." My impoverished drawl combated with his moneyed environment.

I hopped onto the table, straddling his hips and rubbing my glistening cunt against the shaft of his yearning cock. I felt him wriggle beneath me, like a wettened worm.

"I want it to break... inside you." Paul whined. Oh, if I could only tell you how hot that made me.

I made a show of shimmying up his frame until my pelvis was hanging over his face. Delicately, I reached down and massaged the lump. It was as I imagined, inflamed with infection. The flesh was searingly hot to the touch, and his mold was sturdy beneath the skin.

"Do you want mommy to pop your boo-boo?" I asked, matching his baby-talk.

"Yes. Yes, please, mommy!" He simpered.

I lowered myself over him. My vagina touched his grease-mound. The protrusion seemed to inflate beneath me, like a rubber ball being pumped into my cunt.

"Oh, do you want mommy to make you creamy?"

"Please!" Paul whinnied.

I began to twist my hips, working the oversized zit further into my yawning groin. It felt like I was putting a heated rag inside my pussy.

"Here it comes! Here comes... the *pop*!"

I sat down with all my weight.

I felt the spot where the milky-white dewdrop of fluid had appeared first. The creamy contents of his pimple zipped up from that break and filled my cunt. It was like someone had set off a fire extinguisher inside me. White foam, silly-string textured fluids, and jizz-snot burst inside of me all at once.

I began to thrust up and down, my vagina mulching his lump like a toothless mouth. We both exclaimed with joy as I rode his face.

Behind me, I heard him shuck his cock with a frantic hand. He came up the arch of my back, but his dollop of ejaculate did nothing for me. I just wanted to be filled with his sickness.

Then, the table broke from underneath us.

Despite being such a rich bastard, he had really wimped out on the table. It was a plastic piece with foldable legs.

When we slammed into the ground, I drove all my weight into my pelvis. I heard his neck snap and felt warm blood spatter up the crease of my rump.

Quickly, I pulled myself off of him. The deflated sack of skin that had held his treasured juice sloughed out of me like afterbirth.

I cautiously walked away from him, hoping that Paul would stand up and shake the injury off.

His head was bent at an awkward angle, and I could see a bone denting the surface of his neck-meat. The Man was clearly dead... killed in the midst of his obscene ecstasy. Killed doing what he loved most.

My thighs were so slickened with pimple puke, I looked like I had gotten hit with a pie by a perverse clown.

"Damn." I said. "Jus' when it was getting' good too!"

**Epilogue**

I ran out of there butt-naked.

I drove toward home in a panic, not knowing what I was going to say to Mathias. Maybe the butler would send the police after me, or maybe he would remain silent about the whole affair. Did he want people knowing his former employer had died while zit-fucking some skank he met online? Not likely, but I couldn't risk it.

As I drove, I reflected on the facts. Two people had died because of my fetish. Sure, not every pimple-themed sexual encounter indeed in mayhem... but one was more than enough! Two? Two felt unlucky. Two felt like a goddamn pattern.

I swore off sex with strangers as I drove, deciding instead to finally talk to Mathias and admit what I wanted from him. Maybe, after all this time, he wouldn't find it so strange. Maybe... he'll accept me—

My phone buzzed in my cupholder.

I reached over and plucked it up, happy to see that Mathias had left me a text message.

My happiness didn't last long.

"You forgot to delete your browser history". Mathias texted me an hour ago. Then, five minutes ago: "We need to talk".

I gulped, pulled over, and wept on the side of the road. Naked, coated in gunk, and running from a corpse... I felt nothing but shame. My husband had discovered my deepest, darkest secret. There was no putting it back in the box.

I wanted to blame him. It had, after all, been his zits which had goaded this on.

There's no telling what he'll say. Maybe he'll leave me.

## NO ONE RIDES FOR FREE

Maybe he'll tell me that he still loves me... no matter how I get my rocks off.

No matter what... I just wanted to write to y'all and tell you my sordid story first. I know I haven't talked to you guys in a long time, and it's just because I finally found *my* kink, and I wasn't sure if it would be welcomed here.

So, if this story grossed you out and you want nothing more to do with me... I'm okay with that. But if you have some zits you'd like popped and are looking for a partner to do it with ya...

Hit me up.

I'm real easy to find.

I'm the motherfuckin' *Cream Queen*.

NO ONE RIDES FOR FREE

Cover design services for the beautifully creepy. Premades, customs, magazine covers, etc.

Twitter: @grimpoppydesign

Patreon: patreon.com/grimpoppydesign

# NO ONE RIDES FOR FREE

Made in the USA
Coppell, TX
16 May 2025